SILENT
CITY

SARAH DAVIES-GOFF

SILENT CITY

TINDER
PRESS

First published in Great Britain in 2023 by Tinder Press
An imprint of HEADLINE PUBLISHING GROUP

3

Cataloguing in Publication Data is available from the British Library

Hardback ISBN 978 1 4722 5524 2
Trade paperback ISBN 978 1 4722 5525 9

Typeset in Sabon by Avon DataSet Ltd, Alcester, Warwickshire

Printed and bound in Great Britain by Clays Ltd, Elcograf S.p.A.

Headline's policy is to use papers that are natural, renewable and recyclable
products and made from wood grown in well-managed forests and other
controlled sources. The logging and manufacturing processes are expected
to conform to the environmental regulations of the country of origin.

HEADLINE PUBLISHING GROUP
An Hachette UK Company
Carmelite House
50 Victoria Embankment
London EC4Y 0DZ

www.tinderpress.co.uk
www.headline.co.uk
www.hachette.co.uk

For Will, Henry and Sarah, and James

Prologue

TWICE ON THE ROAD, THE LEADERS, MARE AND SENE, take me aside and hit me. *Where are you from? What are you doing out here? Where are your others?* They are not above smacking the bloody hole in my head where my ear used to be.

I try to show them I can take it. Keeping quiet is easy, but I have to use all my fourteen years of strength and experience to not cry. They knock the very speak out of me.

They have questions, but I know who they are. They are banshees.

To me, banshees are heroes. I saw images of banshees growing up at home on the island, women dressed in black, warriors. The ones who fight the skrake. 'Here to Protect' the grimy posters said.

I thought I could be one of them so I set out to find them. And here we are.

The punches come and it's like being hit by a rock. I keep my whisht. I think of the runaways they are after, Cillian, Nic and Aodh, safe on my island to the west, while we work east.

To the banshees, I'm an outsider and not to be trusted. They found me on a beach, fighting for my life and losing. They killed them all, with ease, with grace, while behind me, through the mist on the sea, the runaways escaped. They bind my hands, they question me. They leave my feet free and we move fast.

In the afternoon of that third day the banshees and me come upon the outskirts of the city. They keep moving, smooth and sure, but I am caught standing on a briary slope. Dublin stretches below me, grey and glinting wet. The rain gone and the country fresh. The city like a crust on the green skin of Ireland, a scab flaking slowly away.

If I stop, I know Agata will stop too, but before she finds me I want just one moment alone. I want to feel like I have conquered something, standing here, having found the banshees and the city, and still not dead, and not made a skrake. Not yet, anyway.

I am only tired and frightened. The fight is wore off me on to the road. *Hungry road.* I put my dirty fingers to where my ear used be and dried blood crumbles away. It's still chewing, so it is.

Agata's shadow lands across me and I flinch. She only stares out over the land with an expression I can't make out. It's too big to take in, all the things that happened me. I don't know which way to go with them. Once we're in the city, I know, there'll only be more to try and understand. But it will be over; there will be an ending. I can stop fighting. I can retreat, a little, into the quiet of my own head. Even whether I live or die will be out of my hands, and that feels like a good thing, a necessary thing. A rest.

'There.' Agata points. I follow the line of her finger to a patch of green, the other side of the city and a little inland. 'Phoenix City.'

From this distance nothing but a blur of grey in a sea of green and brown.

'We'll follow a road that circles off around the left,' Agata goes on. 'Keep out of Dublin, it's crawling with skrake.' She is quiet while the last of the banshees pass us.

Nothing surprises me – or, it's that everything is so fucking shocking I've no capacity for surprise any more. I nod to show I hear her. 'What else?'

Agata looks at me and I look back at her and there is something I recognise – grimness, resignation. A nub of something familiar that makes me feel just a little less desolate.

'You'll know all of it soon enough.' She hesitates. 'Don't trust anyone till you know them.'

I let my eyes flicker off back to Dublin.

I don't know you, is what I didn't say. Maybe she is warning me about that as well.

The banshees make a joke out of blindfolding me – they make a joke out of most things.

'You're lucky wearing this,' Lin says to me. 'The last bit isn't pretty.'

'Don't be knifing anything with this on you.'

'Yeah, I like my tits where they are.'

A chorus of 'So do wes', more laughter. I'm getting to know their voices already, all distinct, but even still, keeping track of them gives me a headache.

'It's so stupid,' Lin says. 'There's no point to it.'

'Management says,' Mare tells her.

'Tsss. Management, who haven't been out the walls since.'

'Since ever,' Aoife says. She takes Lin's side, partly because Lin is her partner and partly because otherwise Lin would be alone. This I know already.

Still, nobody stops what they are doing.

The blindfold – a black cloth, damp and musty – is pulled tight and I sink into darkness. It's almost a relief. The banshees spin me till I'm dizzy and it works: I've no idea where we came from. I still know where we are headed, though.

The banshees jostle me along.

It is tough going at first, but they surround me, bumping me along the right way, too close to me to let me fall. I put one foot in front of the other, same as ever. I listen hard, but not to them. A rustle of wind in trees and then of rubbish in streets. The banshees are quiet for a stretch and I hear, far off, the screams of skrake.

Down, then up, and then steeply down again. It becomes cold and damp feeling. An enclosed space, and then we are up to our knees in water. After a long time we stop, and I hear a great wrenching of metal against stone. The air is putrid. We move forwards and the same wrenching again, behind me. Some kind of gate.

We come up again and I feel a breeze of fresher air. At last there are voices, and I'm pushed on faster. Rough hands, not Agata's, but Sene's and Mare's. I can feel her, though; she is still with me. The blindfold itches my nose and I go to rub it with my shoulder. Out of nowhere a hit, hard, in the back of the head. It is easy to let the tears well behind a blindfold at least. Being hit in the dark hurts worse.

I am stopped, at last, with strong hands put squarely on my shoulders. A noise, the first I can identify in a while other than voices, breathing and footsteps. We are outside still but, with the way the sounds of the banshees bounce off walls, I can feel buildings are close by.

It is a fight not to drop to my knees with pure exhaustion. I try to lock them upright, to lift my chin, roll my head on my neck. The banshees surround me.

The noise is a thumping, nearly rhythmic. I think I can smell skrake, but there is no sense of panic around me. I try again to relax my shoulders, to let go a little. Breathe.

The blindfold is whipped away without a word and I blink into the gloom.

'Night.' A woman's voice. *Thump, thumb thump.* A swish. 'Best time to train.' I blink again and the world comes into focus a little better. 'Only time for me, usually.'

She huffs out a couple of breaths.

'Ash,' Mare whispers, bowing her head.

'An outlier. She's not bound?' Ash sounds impatient.

I look around. We are standing in a big square, the buildings on each side looming in the dark. Glowering nearly. Packed dirt beneath my feet. It's hard to see much.

'No, Mother,' Mare says, so quiet her voice just barely reaches through the air.

I watch Ash, fascinated, forgetting about my exhaustion.

Her hair is long for a banshee, and she is taller even than Sene. She lets loose a flurry at her punching bag, a jab jab cross, a jab jab uppercut cross and there is something so gorgeous and generous and powerful about her. She finishes with a spinning kick from a standing start and her form is perfect, the force, the height she manages.

She is the biggest person I've ever seen, her shoulders rounded, her thighs and upper arms powerful. She walks gracefully, each step managed carefully by dainty, pointed feet. Not a bit out of breath as she comes towards us, unwrapping her hand guards. 'And the others?'

I am glad she is looking at Mare so I can continue to gape at her.

Suddenly, a rush of activity.

From the other side of the square, coming at us—

Skrake. I knew it.

There are no discernable thoughts. I run past Ash, pushing her aside with all my might, out of the path of the skrake. My hand goes for my last knife, still hidden in its sheath on my ankle, my mother's knife.

I ground myself and aim, and it is coming so fast, straight for us. I let fly.

Somewhere between aiming and firing I get a look. It is a big one. It had been a large man once, and there are still wisps of hair attached to the scalp. Something wrong with the jaw or what was the jaw: it is hanging off to the side with the skrake's proboscis, a huge slug-like organ, sliming fully out of its body and up through its mouth. The smell. Once bitten, it will take a week, maybe two, to die. It's painful. The life shitting out of you. But instead of you just dying, the skrake takes up your body and uses it like a puppet. Fast, vicious, strong, with long sharp teeth, the skrake is like a child's bad dream.

The skrake goes down about ten foot from where we stand. It is not dead. I know that already. I have to move – the fear is beginning to set on me – but I find my wrists are held tight behind my back.

Ash holds me absolutely still in front of her while the monster rights itself and comes at us, all dead flesh and teeth, and the handle of my knife up to the hilt in its eye-socket.

I'm going to die, I think. All this way, I came through so much and now this . . .

The skrake stops, its jaws going like mad. A metal collar around its neck, its arms. It is held entirely by chains.

8

Ash's punching bag.

She lets go my hands and I stumble backwards, never taking my eyes off the skrake.

'I go out and bring one back every now and then,' she says, smiling as she walks over to the skrake. Ash casually plucks my knife from its eye, expertly avoid its roving hands, the jaw still trying to snap, though it has fallen half off. She wipes off the blade of my knife on a length of fabric at her belt.

'I'm going to take care of this for you,' she says, and she lets that warm smile fall directly on me while I sit in the dirt. While my last good knife disappears like the rest.

'I like this one, Mare,' she calls, grinning.

'Let's keep her.'

The City

Six Years Later

ANOTHER GLORIOUS DAY IN PHOENIX CITY.

Another night made of fitful sleep, waking in the dark, thinking I hear my mother crying for me to come home.

The banshees are up with the sun, the vapours of our dirty breaths mingling together in the shitty air. We dress, as best we can, in various shades of black, the best and darkest clothes on the oldest and wiliest of us. Layers, where we can find them; wraps for our wrists and ankles and breasts. Feet stay bare for the most part; we've shoes, but they're only for missions, and for the latrines. Dressing is ritual, for banshees. There's an art to the way styles are mixed, there's ingenuity and guile. We check each other, encourage, edit.

Agata is finishing wrapping her hands, shaking her head at me. 'Bad bitch,' she sighs quietly. We put our foreheads together for a moment, letting our breaths mingle, then we're going.

Our dorm is three storeys up, and the noise of the morning is our bare feet on the stone blocks of the stairs, a slapping smooth sound, sending aches into our already cold flesh.

There's something about that building, with its echoes and smells and the broken windows. There's a rhythm I can nearly make out every morning, a patter of us working together, working towards something for-ever just out of reach while whatever is coming up behind us – famine, disease, the skrake – inches closer.

There are worse ways to wake up, so there are. I've seen them.

This building was once a hospital. There's the name of it outside the front on a sign, the letters carved deep into stone. I try to see it as it might have been when it was meant to bring comfort and help to people. The little rooms with the painful-looking equipment, the long, echoing corridors.

Nothing in this building heals now. Banshees do not

save anything; we do not bring succour. This is what I have learned.

Whatever whispers of conversation were starting up, warming us into the day, they are cut short on the threshold of the dorms. The city is silent. They'd cut the tongues out of the very dogs. If there were any dogs left. No talking in-house unless it can't be helped, no talking at all when we're under the sky, no clanging, no messing, no slipping.

That slapping of our own feet against the ground when we're out running is the only noise a person who is not a banshee will hear out of us some days. If they're lucky.

We don't need to talk to each other anyway. We know each other's thoughts, we know what jokes Aoife wants to make, which direction Mare will turn us next, we know where Lin's appraising eye will fall.

Out the back is where we are. The building looms up around on four sides and I can't help but Beware.

Beware tall . . .

I'm shrugging it off, my shoulders the same slippery stone of the dorm stairs. The voices of my mothers, warnings from a lifetime ago. I keep trying to leave them behind. Beware tall buildings in case they fall down on you is the learning they drilled into me. One piece amongst many.

The buildings around us make a box, a place for our morning stretches and afternoon sparring sessions. This area houses nearly all the banshees, except those few high enough to have made management, or to be protecting management, over in Government Buildings. Real beds over there is what I've heard. Someone told me there's taps you can turn on and water will run out, clean and cold. You can bathe in the stuff.

As we file out, the night-watch start in. Red-eyed but alert still, silent on their feet, cold as hell despite the extra rations of clothes. I nod at Saoirse, Sanchez, Yen and the rest of B-Troop. Ahead of me, Agata has her hand out to touch them home in a friendly manner, but Saoirse goes to dig her instead and Agata lets her hand drop. I go for her – I can't help it. A great leap in the air, a powerful spin-kick going straight for Saoirse's smug little face, but Mare, out of nowhere, throws one of her long legs out to rein me in.

Awful pricks, B-Troop.

Agata's hand is on my shoulder. I glance at her and she gives a wink. She doesn't let it bother her. Tough and relaxed and I love her. It annoys me, though. There's no need to let these pricks push us around.

We're getting going, together and correct, a team. First in the troop leads, and Second enforces, but Mare and Sene don't need to tell us anything. Stretches done, but we're only getting cooler in the still morning air. We get them over quick and easy, and we get moving.

We're running.

We move in our twos, headed out of the hospital complex for the north face of the wall. The limbs are slow and solid-feeling. It's difficult to move for the first click or so but we work at it. Getting our feet to hit the ground light, we work on our silence and our speed. We're running and, beside me, Agata, familiar as my own skin, coughs, hucks up something and spits it elegantly off to her left.

There's a great brick wall still surrounding the city. On this side of the wall, the city side, there is a trench thirty foot deep and nearly as wide. The earth is taken and used to build up a tall bank, shadowing the wall and reinforcing it, the whole way around the city. The sides are soft with grass. Plants have done their best to grow up out of the earth on either side, and I look at them, thinking: me too. Farmers try to get crops out of it, sorghum and potatoes but, for all their effort, there are children starving in the city. The bank of the wall is so thick on top you can use it to look over the other side, down at the skrake if you want to, or run on it, the full twelve click circumference of the city. Every day we run it.

Sometimes we run the wall counter-clockwise to try

keep things fresher in our stagnant little training pool. When we reach the wall, we turn left, six of us moving together soft and quick in the cold early morning. Behind us another troop follows on. There's something in the way Mare and Sene move this morning, I think. We're on a run but we're going somewhere. There's some little mission to be done. My heart sinks.

I watch my feet; the top here is uneven. This wall is a monument to the hundreds of thousands that've worked these city barriers since Phoenix became what it is now – refuge, last stand. Open wound. The last remnants of everything that was wrong before the Emergency, as well as those few bits that were right and worth hanging on to.

The skrake are out there, over the other side, or the shrayke, shriek, Z or Zee, as they were known back when. Slugs, monsters, the Emergency, the ruin, gnashers, plain old fuckface. Nearly as many monsters in here as there are out there, is what Agata tells me. She's right, I'd say.

Even with the quiet of the city, they can hear us, or smell us. All the quiet in the world doesn't matter much when we're all here together, stinking up the air so deliciously, with management throwing them a live one every few months. And us helping.

To my right, over the wall, they stand three deep.

Four or more in places, pressing in, jostling against each other to get close. Mostly naked now, the people they once were are flayed away till there's nothing left but mouth and teeth and slug-proboscis-tongue. Reaching for us.

Just one could end it all. They've got in before, though not in living memory. Stories passed down: lessons. We've all lost someone to the skrake.

Our troop comes upon the wallers about two clicks into our run. We meet them every day at some part of the wall, depending on our route and theirs. They're never resting, but every day working like their lives depend on it, even the children. You can see their bones through whatever threadbare clothing they wear, held together by stitches we can nearly count as we go past. Some of them have shovels, some are using smaller tools or just pointed sticks to help break up the hard-packed earth. The children use their hands on the muck, their little fingers cold. It hurts to watch, and the city solves that by never looking at them.

The wallers dig the trench deeper, make it neater, constantly reinforcing the wall. They work day and night, looked over by a few pairs of banshees, watching and swinging their sticks lazily. A gang leader for each section keeps them at it. One shift from the rising of the sun to its going down gets you one day's rations.

You'd eat three times what they give you working that wall. This, while management are red in the face exerting themselves with nonsense about how nobody starves in this city as long as they're willing to 'contribute'.

I glance back at Aoife under cover of spitting, and she's watching the wallers too, her eyes soft. She'd better not let anyone else see her eyes like that, so she'd not. I click my teeth quietly and she comes to, glances up at me and away again, her expression blank again.

A few of the wallers look up at us running by, eyes huge in their pinched faces, shining, and you could nearly cod yourself they're looking at you in admiration. In others, the women maybe especially, it's just plain fear.

There's a special stink you get down here, distinct from our own, and at whatever bit of the wall they're working on. The skrake are six deep instead of three. That's what you get when you don't pause in your work, when a little noise is a necessary part of what you do. Apart from us, the wallers get closer to the skrake than anyone else in this dark city, in their unending work to put more soil and more wall and more bricks and stones between us and the outside. At the end of each shift – a day or a night – they're told to go home as if they have homes to go to. Dwellings in the shanties, maybe, some of them. Others not even that, and all with hungry bellies. The hardest work in the city, though

17

the farmers think it is theirs. The banshees even think we have it the worst, and the breeders and everything in between. Management – I can't get into what management might be thinking.

We're warming up, anyway. That first click, the scramble up to the wall, the getting out on top of it and falling into line, that's always the worst, but we're all right now, we're awake and alert. Once we're past the wallers, Mare and Sene will ease up a little.

Stories are still told of the last time the wall came down – a part of it, anyway. Most of the wallers were killed, and killed first. By the time they'd a handle on it, hundreds were dead, a good part of the city population. The few that survived were those lucky enough to have stairs to run up and doors to close. Banshees died along with the rest, and some of the older ones are still sore with the wallers about it, as if they opened a door for the skrake.

Management blamed wallers, too. There aren't many ways worse to go than getting bit, but I'd say they'd have gone looking if the wallers weren't all dead already. It's a dangerous job even without the fear of the skrake getting on top of you. There's the heat in the day and the cold at night. There're even stories of kids drowning in the ditches after a big rain. You'd think they'd look out for each other better down there.

I check myself.

They're pure exhausted. If anyone should be watching out for them, finding ways to protect, it should be us. It should be, and it isn't. When management say we're for 'security', they do not mean security for everyone. They mean security *against* everyone.

On we run, going a good pace now, and we're out to a long blank stretch of wall where we can ease into ourselves. A little over four clicks down and just the eight now ahead of us. This is where I really start to think about the thirst. I swallow thickly against my breath and keep on going. There's something about moving in this way, the methodical clean functioning of tired but obedient limbs, about training past tiredness, that feels like home to me. It takes the long line between the present and my past, growing up on an island far to the west, with only my mother who bore me and Maeve, who trained me, and it balls it right up, makes it nothing.

Up ahead of us now to the Broken Finger and on we keep. That uncomfortable little twinge in my side starts up again and I've an urge to pause and rub it, but there's no pausing on morning runs and nothing I can do but keep on, not let the team down. It'll ease up.

I should mention it to Agata. I don't want secrets building up between us. I should tell her about the dreams calling me home.

It'll ease up.

A person could injure herself unnecessarily and there are other ways to show toughness, to get them to see the grit you have, but these ways are not up to me. Stiff and all as I am, I'm grateful not to be the one to have to try and figure out our futures. I've no love for management but there they are, running the city. I wince and feel Agata beside me stiffen up a little and watch me, but on we go. Nothing to be done. Plenty worse things going on in the city.

More people milling around now as the day begins to age. I see a lumbering shape, moving in an odd, slow way. It's management. You can tell because of the good clothes and the haughtiness of him, even from here. He's got sticks under both arms and he's using them to move his legs along, which seem nearly useless to him. Not the first one I've seen moving around like this.

Up a little and then relief as we slow to a jog and then a walk. Here are the great doors of the city, half as tall as the buildings at our base. Closed for aeons. Thick wood, and only room for one banshee to go over them at a time, so we make a little line on the thick catwalk of planks, hands lightly on the guard rails, to wait for each other on the other side before running on again in formation.

Downhill now a little towards the shanties.

There is a gate here too, a working one with a lock and a key. Above the gate in thick stone lettering it says 'Dublin Zoo', but mostly it's called the shanties because of the types of dwelling that people use here – sheets of whatever is to hand put up against each other at right angles. The zoo is big, and we aren't called down there much. There, they're expected to make their own way, unless they're caught for something in Phoenix proper. We've been there, our troop, to serve the city's justice, but I never learned my way around. It's twisty, there are buildings, big pools of mud, huge plastic screens, intact still, despite everything. For the animals that were kept.

We run on by, following the great city wall. The further south we get, the more wretched people look, and the shanties are the most southern spot in the city. Here there are skinnier, dirtier people crammed around the cook-fires: those that can't work, can't find a place for themselves, or so management would have it.

Still they try and live, and are allowed to do so, for the most part. For a city apparently so interested in pro-tecting life, they don't mind when it's lost down here. No water or food rations for belonging to such and such house, unless you go to the wall or maybe get work as a runner, which is only for the young and healthy and determined, or maybe as a cleaner or cook. They'd still have to come to sleep and survive down here at the end of the day.

I try to imagine it the way it was before I came. The city walls were fit to burst with people, but the breeders were working full time to make more, the whip of the hopes of the management on them.

Then the sickness. The way the banshees whisper about it, the stillness in their faces, tells how bad it was. It took a while to notice maybe, the shits being so common here. But people started not being able to make it even to these trenches. They'd shit themselves in the streets, in their beds. They wouldn't be able get up from where they lay. Everything they ate, whatever they could get to drink, ran right out of them, dark and hot, streaming their lives away. They faded out of the world, the last with no one to look after them or hold their hands or fight for something to drink for them. I can imagine it well. You'd know from the look people get when they talk about it. They're frightened of times like them coming again.

The shanties were blamed and cordoned off: the great metal fence – made to keep in the animals they used to show off, surrounding the whole of the shanties – was mended, and the huge gates – with 'Zoo' written over the top still – closed and bolted. Till then, the command had been, and is now, that the gate stay open to facilitate the banshees coming and going to guard the entrance to the tunnel, the only way out of the city. And then, banshees stood guard to try and protect the better-offs up the hill. Who is to say it even started down there? They won't speak at all about the clean-up, so they won't. I try to imagine it, taking the bodies, caked in their own shit still, whatever friends or family, their children, left crying after them, their own bellies like fire. And then going through whatever belongings they'd amassed. That's what I'd do, I know that for sure. You learn all kinds of things about yourself here.

The bodies were not permitted to remain in the city, so the banshees carried them over to the finger and threw them off. Wearing, as usual, whatever protections they could get hold of against the corpses, which were not even wrapped. Winter always on its way.

It's here we're headed, I realise now: a change in the camber ahead of us and we veer down, off the wall and towards the huge gates.

They're closed.

These gates are meant to stay open. There's nowhere in the city we should be barred from, unless management say so.

We pull up and Mare doesn't need to tell us what to do. Aoife and Lin take a side each and pull. When the gates don't give, Agata and I give a hand, Sene and Mare, too. I watch as I strain against the weight of them, the bulk of Mare's smooth dark biceps curving beautifully beside me. The gates take a minute to give and I look up, trying to think how hard it'd be to scale them. Then there's the squeal of metal on metal and they open; we pull till they're wide.

I'm hoping we can just turn round now and head back, but that's not how these things go. The twang in my side pinches dramatically and I twitch against the pain. Agata glances at me and I think of her, again, holding me back off fighting that gobshite Saoirse. Her and Mare. Protecting me, not against getting beat but against the wrath of management for dealing one out.

I'll tell her. I can tell her anything.

We are heading into the shanties and it's the same old shit: metal sheets, planks of wood, previous bits of plastic, placed at right angles till they might help cover you from cold. The elderly, the sick. Children. How they survive down here with few to work, nobody fit enough to wall or farm or skiv – and then us, and banshees like us, coming down to make things more difficult.

I harden myself. They made things more difficult for themselves.

We go for the centre, but it doesn't really matter where we're aiming for. We're here to send a message, and as long as it's clear enough, everyone down here will see it.

Mare and Sene make for a gathering of hovels and, with a nod, Agata and I are set loose. I take a metal sheet and pull, kicking to make it harder to use again. Inside the dwelling is a woman, her arms wide and her eyes full of terror – but she clamps her mouth tight to keep in any shouts of fear or alarm or anger.

Together we pull and wreck till the place is flattened, Agata going maybe hardest of all.

I block my mind against it all, feeling nothing, thinking nothing.

Once we have done enough ruining, once the punishment is big enough, Mare gives the signal and we go to leave. I follow on, giving the place a final lookabout, satisfying myself there's nothing handy we can bring off with us. Used be you could loot some useful bits down here.

I give a final glance back to see the woman crouch over a gathering of rubbish and fabric, exposed now to the elements. Inside is a girl, just a few years old, scrawny and wild-haired. She watches us leave, her skinny arms wrapped around the neck of her mother. Her eyes huge.

I linger. It's a mistake.

'Help,' the mother says, her dark hair plastered against her scalp, the scar of a burn on one cheek.

I look around: the other banshees making their way out towards the gate again, the ruins of this woman's home forgotten.

The mother crying silently, her eyes entreating me, while the girl shivers in her arms.

I open my mouth to say something but the words lodge in my throat. All I can do is go.

Near the gate, looking around numbly, I see an odd, very old thing: a poster, rigged up to a stick like a flag. An image of banshees on it, faceless, dressed in black, moving in twos. 'Fighting for You', it says.

The Barracks

B Y THE TIME WE'RE BACK, SWEATING AND THIRSTY, the fires are hot and there's water for us, still warm from the boil and cloudy, but ready to drink. It grows on you, so it does. After a while you can't taste it or smell it. I lost two teeth these first few years in the city, and it's sore to press down fully with my jaw. A lot of the goodness, the pure strong health I had, is gone out of me.

We're all dying here, dying slow unless we're dying quick.

I can't stop thinking about the woman with the burns and her girl. I try to shake it off. It's nothing I haven't seen seven times a week in this city. Every time

I close my eyes they're there, asking me for help.

It's my favourite part of the day, usually, with the run over, getting back into the yard with my troop, the warm feeling amongst us. We stretch out, and I try not to think about the way that little girl looked in her mother's arms. As if someone could just reach out and change their lives.

A lot not to think about here in this city; a lot to close yourself off from.

We're quiet, of course, but I listen out. There's the noise of feet on cold packed ground, breathing, the homely sound of fabric against skin. I shuffle up the queue, stretching my neck back so I can see the tops of the cold buildings on each side of our yard, twisting to each corner of the rectangular space, keeping an eye out for B-Troop, though they should be sleeping after their night shift. The line moves slowly. At the top I nod to the woman behind the big dirty pot, take my drink and have three long swallows. My headache is nudged back a little. At my usual sitting-place I rest my back against the stones and close my eyes, cooling down already. I gulp the air. Mare will move us inside in a minute. Agata sits next to me. She doesn't touch me, I don't open my eyes, but I know it all the same. We'll go in a minute to the dining hall, but for now there's fresh air, light, space.

My first days here, all this was impossible; being surrounded by people, being surrounded by walls. The life in me would just go out. I'd throw my arms around my head and lie on the ground and just – panic. When I first came here I could only deal with things in small bits. Everywhere was unknown and unsafe: the building, our dorm, the corridors, our training square. The place we gather to eat was the hardest place. The first time I went with Agata and the banshees to this eating-place, fresh in from the country, I had some kind of stop in my head.

I remember first seeing those long stone corridors. Not much light. The quiet chatter of the banshees around us, the slapping of feet on the flagstones, the shadows on the walls. Always the smell. It was enough to be dealing with, so it was, and there was a pressure building behind my eyes, an angry fuzz.

The busyness of the kitchens up ahead of us and I could feel it like a thunder starting out ahead of me on the horizon. There was a problem ahead but, still and all, my feet kept moving forwards. That's how it often goes, I'm finding.

We went through one door and another, my heart going so fast I worried it might do me damage, feeling like it'd just jump on up out of my throat. The dining room, when we got to it, was huge. Three long windows, all with glass, throwing in good light. That day was warm from the sunlight coming in, heating it up, and the warmth of all the bodies as well. There're tables – six long ones – and chairs around all of them, wood and wire, and some long benches and stools as well. Most of this I couldn't take in that first day, or the next, or the ones after that.

I'd say it is the noise, but there're nearly no voices you can hear. It's the smell, the odour of roasted food. The reek of bodies, of breath, of unclean hair, hot armpits and groins and feet. The revolting gathered *meat* of people. Eyes and noses and lips and hair, all separate textures, different skins wrapping it all up – for now. The shapes of the shoulders and the arms and the legs. The hands, no two the same. All the different ways they have of moving, each a way I have not seen before and mightn't see again, each in a pose and a light that'll only last a moment.

What gets in the way of my taking it all in is that it's just too fucking *much*, this building with its rooms and its people and its sleeping-places and dark corridors and noises and smells, and its feeling of cold, of repressed noise. The people in it, the banshees, are the thing my head has to get in around and past, and for the longest time it can *not*. It does not.

There was a break in my mind that first day and lots of others besides, a refusal, a closing off. Walking into the room, I was confronted with too many bodies, carried along with the movement of the banshees accompanying me. I couldn't stop my eyes from darting around, from trying to absorb every detail, every texture and colour. Heart jumping still like I'd seen a skrake, breath short and shallow. I could not seem to draw the one deep breath I needed, and then there was someone trying to whisper to me, to ask me something, but all I heard was buzzing, growing louder, and then, all around the edges of where I was looking, a darkness.

Darkness coming in on top of me.

I was gone.

Out. Off. Done till I woke up with Agata's cool hand in mine.

Agata was the only one that could help me. She'd stay back and give me space and time to breathe. She waited for me. Her expression soft, open, making a place for me to come in to when I was ready. Keeping me in open spaces when she could.

I know it a little better now. I can watch for the signs and go back outside, breathe slow, close my eyes, place myself where I am. Things happen to us physically, and our minds are part of that too.

This is what comes of growing up on an island in the west with only two people ever to look at, two people to know. And not just that, but what happened to them –

losing them, painfully, one then the other. My black dog then too, leaving me nobody. My heart torn out from me again and again, but I could keep going.

Until a roomful of women undid me.

Punishment

TWO WOMEN WAIT. AN OLDER WOMAN AND A younger woman. It is dark but they feel the light coming.

They are nearly as cold as the air itself. There is nothing to give them away. Their naked feet as tough as the packed earth beneath them, their scant clothes requiring their very skin to be their armour.

They hear him before they see him: his boots, crunching on the ice and mud, the luxurious rustle of cloth against cloth. He never had cause to be as quiet as these women.

There is an inky black against the gentle blue of the night.

A man walking home alone.

He has tucked himself into so many clothes against the night air that only his nose is visible. So much fabric; riches.

He's breathing heavily, leaving a trail of hot air and a rich-feeling smell as he walks slowly towards his own part of the city.

They knew he would take a quiet path, away from the main road, though even that would be deserted at this time of the night. They have been here with him before. They knew he'd be shuffling as if he'd no cause to fear. He never has had cause before.

The women are silent, their toes choosing the spots of ground where they won't slip or squelch or crack ice.

The path curves slowly around to the left. At first there's nowhere much to hide and, careless and all as the man is, they leave long stretches where they can barely see him. But as they get to management quarters the buildings thicken and the women get closer.

There's room sometimes in these quiet, dark corridors of power. There are places where might can be wrung out and turned over. For a few moments, at least.

The man is close to home now and hurrying, impatient for his clean bed and warm blankets.

Curling around the brick and stone houses, the women arrange themselves around him, just like they practised.

With a burst of speed, they make their move.

The younger woman steps in front of him, smiling a small smile under her hood, her lips stretching against the cold. The man stops short in surprise. He is not afraid. He thinks she has made a mistake; he thinks that he has found her in a dark alley. He leers and deliberates before taking a step towards her. The older woman moves silently, still unseen, behind him.

The man is unwrapping the soft fabric muffled around his neck and mouth to say—

Nothing, nothing comes out but a gasp of air. The older woman has taken a length of wire and she has reached around his head and pulled hard so it is tight against his neck.

The women work together to handle him from the path and around a corner. The man's skin is slippy with blood where the flesh of his neck is being cut into. He has not drawn a full breath for some moments, but the woman with the wire does not let up.

The older woman would saw his head clean away from his shoulders, but that's not the plan. A luxury of space, she is thinking. This is what it does for them up here. Nobody around to see anything. She feels so strongly that she can, that she *should* pull more tightly and finish him for good that her muscles ache with the effort of restraint.

The older woman can feel the eyes of her partner on her, half warning and half smiling, and she relents, letting the man take a breath before drawing the wire a little tighter again. Her partner's eyes flick away, wanting already to be done, to be moving away. The younger woman is very experienced at hurting people. Someone she can learn from.

She lets up the wire and lets him draw another lungful. The control is delicious. She wants to see the transformation she knows will come, and when the man begins to whimper and beg with the little air she's giving him, she feels relief, a short satisfaction. Something she suspected was true and is here in front of her. He is revealed. All true ends are revelations, she thinks.

Her partner now holds something sharp. She grasps each of his legs one at a time and makes long, deep cuts. The man tries to scream but cannot.

The older woman, the one with the wire, stays where she is, thinking hard, her excited breath pumping warmth into the night air. She's pressing harder than she means to, her hands with a life of their own, yet not nearly as hard as she would like. She wants so badly to end it now.

Then, a breath in the night, her partner at her ear whispering.

'What's coming for him will be worse.'

She lets go of her wire and the man crumples to the frozen ground, bleeding hard from the backs of his legs and a little from his neck, struggling for breath. She steps forwards, grabs the edge of a great swathe of fabric protecting his body and pulls hard.

He will be hoarse for weeks, and he will never walk again.

The attack took moments.

They were quicker than the last time, and next time they'll be even faster still.

The younger woman wraps the fabrics around them both and together the women slip away through the dark.

Justice

I DREAM OF MY MOTHERS, THEIR VOICES MINGLING with the *shinaun*, the constant wind, calling me as if they're beckoning me home after a day's play. I dream of being loved.

I wake.

This morning it's worse than usual, waking up to the city's dark and particular quiet. The bleakness whenever I stop is harder to ignore because of the day that is ahead of us.

I glance at Agata. I am loved, I remind myself. She gives me a blank nod, rallies with a smile.

I get moving quickly to keep off the bad feelings, of being hungry, thirsty, dirty and sticky, of being, just –

sad. And to keep off the thoughts of our morning's work. I get stiffly up out of the lips of my bed and land my bare feet on the cold stone floor.

I slept well even with the dreams, and I'm ashamed of myself.

There's quiet around me despite the noise of so many people living in one small space – no hum of whispers, no hushed laughter. The banshees are holding their breaths. The city holds its breath too. We are all together, on punishment mornings, retreating to our routines so we don't have to think. That is the point of them, is what Agata says. I glance towards her again but she's gone – up and out already.

She used to wait for me in the old days, my first days here. I used to wish she wouldn't.

I get out of our little block room ahead of the other four and go along the corridor, up the stairs, through the hall to the outside. There's a great breath to be had here, of air and light. It's only once you're out that you realise what a stink we make in our squalid little cells. Rubbing my heels into my eyes, yawning, I make for the water troughs and douse myself well, the gritty brown water holding on to the cold of the night. Bracing. The latrine then, but I remember I've no shoes and I jog back, my bare feet slapping against earth and then the cool stones and the whack of the smell, of strong piss, old sweat, sex, unwashed clothes and sour hunger. Ear wax.

I keep my head down and get my shoes on me and run back up and out again, holding it with concentration and pure muscle till I've come around the banshee blocks towards the scrubby patch of earth the latrines rotate in. I squelch in the mud up the hill and squat. Relief.

It's early.

We've yet done nothing that cannot be undone.

We're just doing what we're told, what we have to do. Isn't that why I came here, not to have to think so much? Not to have to be frightened all the time. To be strong and let someone point me in a direction.

In the training square yesterday, after we sparred and were beginning to think of our beds, word came down. A punishment. We are never told who'll be punished or why, till management gives the big speech, and even then, things are vague. The banshees don't feel too concerned, and someone from B-Troop even hoots in approval, wanting a look at the city's new leader.

The only reason to be first out of the blocks in the morning is the little bit of solitude out here in the latrines. Or second, after Agata, but she's off. Wherever she goes off to now. Mornings, in the middle of the night sometimes. And me, not telling her about the girl I saw, the pain in my side. I don't really know how to put words to those things, anyway. The two of us keeping anything back from each other is . . . It's . . . I don't have a word for it. It is not good.

At the back of the block square building, the rough patches of greenery about it, the trees off to my left are nearly the last in the whole city. That'll be it then, this winter, and we'll have to find out some other thing to burn. Furniture. Books. That'll be the last of it. Sounds like B-Troop think the new leader will have answers.

I think it's all crumbling. It has been since well before I arrived here.

My shoes are crumbling. Too small to start with, they've their tips hacked off, and my toes, long and dirty, peek out forlornly unless I scrunch them up, which I do now against the cold and dirt. I got the shoes for a loaf of bread they baked down in the zoo. I got the bread for loot from outside on a mission about a year ago, a pull-around, still in its packet.

I list for myself all the things I'd like. A clean shitting-hole all to myself, the sound of waves, my knives, coddle, a fire in a hearth, my own bedroom with a bed with sheets, sharp scissors, a clean towel, a river to bathe in or the sea, a whole day spread ahead of me with nobody in it. My knives, my knives.

You've to be careful, so you do, even letting yourself

think of the things you want. The mind runs to sad, dark places.

Finished, check with an extra push – no, that's it – and I'm up and moving again, just as others begin making their slippy way up the hill. I look for the shovel but yesterday there was shit somehow on the handle so nobody is covering. This is how we get sick. Even knowing it, all I do is I kick a little earth over and go gingerly, toe-scrunchedly, back down the slope.

A wash. More warm water given every time there's a punishment. Allow us to clean ourselves before we're sullied again.

I walk back to barracks, letting my toes unclench once I'm past the worst bits of the latrines. The fire has been lit in the three big braziers in our square. I nod at the woman tending one and she nods back respectfully, eyes lowered. Six odd years of seeing her and we have never spoken. Women – breeders, skivs, even the children – do not tend to talk much to banshees anyway. We are enforcers. We traditionally aren't here to help. Not the likes of her.

I'm first so I get a good go at washing myself, as well as I can with water that stinks and no soap at all. I dress: the guards and wraps, the head coverings we sometimes use on duty, and Agata joins me and gives me her blandest, friendliest look. Not a word on where she's been, where she goes. I say nothing to her and the distance between us grows.

We get ready for our day's work in the city.

They gather us at the Broken Finger, at the south-east wall of the city, near the shanties of the zoo.

The whole of Phoenix City must once have been overlooked by the finger, a great stone monolith, a hundred times taller and wider than any tree. Once it stood up straight, like a giant's finger pointing up towards the sky. Now, it lies broken on its side, pointing west as if it wants out. Steps made from bricks and rubble lead up to a small standing place at its foot. This standing place gives way then to the finger, tapered towards its end. The end of the finger sticks right over the city walls, hanging high over the skrake below.

The strangest-looking thing in the city. Imagine what people would be at, that they'd had the time to gather and shape all the stones, put them one on top of each other, to make this obscenity, only for it to fall over on them. They'd someone at their backs to make sure they'd the work done, I'd say. Probably they were on starvation rations as well. You wonder how much changes. You wonder how far we've the capacity for it.

And, over the wall, always the skrake, decaying but never dying. Surrounding us, despite the quiet of the city.

It won't be quiet today. Today they'll get fed.

It's starting. I can make out figures in the distance, banshees bringing whoever is being punished down from the basements they have in management.

The hands will be bound, the head covered with a sack. It's hard to tell how well they'll walk, whoever they are. There will be fresh-faced, eager-eyed banshees on either side, pulling and steering along. They're going slow, letting the gathered crowd do their work.

It's the only time the city is all together. People stand roughly according to their importance. Management first, in a circle at the base of the broken plinth surrounded by the Guard, their personal banshees. Can tell them a mile away with their good clothes, best in the city besides management's. Then the higher-up ordinaries, the House Mothers, and breeders, and after those the less important.

See how we honour women, management is saying, in giving us our places next to justice here, as if we are exalted. As if we never are ordered to take women, girls, by the hair to management buildings. A task I've been spared, but for how long? Agata and the others, banshees on the make – we hear the stories from the older banshees. I believe them.

Beyond, off the steps and lining the path to the road, are the farmers, and beyond them the cleaners and the wallers. The shanties then, coming last. And whoever else finding space where they can, surviving however they can. There's what Agata calls 'a strict social hierarchy' here, but it's rough, too. People sneak in around the edges.

Banshees, the Guard usually, will be patrolling the rest of the city and if you're found when you're meant to be here, contributing to the punishment, it won't go well.

At the very top of the plinth stands our new leader, Boyle. The latest to have risen through the ranks with machinations maybe Agata could imagine but I can't. There's so little I understand about the way the city works, I, who came here hardly having seen a man before. The way people work in big groups will always be mysterious to me. But I know the leader is always from management. I could hardly tell one of them apart from another. The last one came to his end here months ago. Usually doesn't take so long for a new one to emerge; the fights they must be having up there.

Makes no odds anyway, who ends up winning power struggles to stand up here before us. Nothing changes, not for the better. I have heard of Boyle's promises of reform and better city discipline and I'm not sure how those promises are so different from his predecessors', or how anyone in management thinks more punishments will save us. There's been talk of more missions, too, and B-Troop are delighted, whispering about it, thinking, I suppose, that if they're obedient enough they'll get made into Guards one day. This punishment will have been Boyle's idea, I realise. A greeting from him to the city, a flex of his new powers.

I stand next to him.

Everyone is taking their places, a long way down the line. There's a lot of waiting on punishment days. I concentrate on breathing out; I look around me while I try not to look like I'm looking.

You can see a lot of the city from up here on the Broken Finger. The highest point of the city at the north-western part of Phoenix, where management dwell in the best buildings, made of stone, made hundreds of years ago to last. The lowest is in the south-east. Shit runs downhill, they say.

Desperate scrawns fan out below us. Gaunt faces, shivering limbs, eyes sunken and defeated. I keep an eye out for the girl and her mother from the shanty we destroyed. I wonder why we did it: who made the order, what that skinny young woman had done to deserve being terrorised, and her child, too. I want to know that she's OK. The city isn't big now, but probably I'll never see her again.

There was a scourge of some kind the year before I came here, and then another last winter. They say our numbers are down. At their height, years ago, there'd have been ten thousand souls in the city, plenty of breeders and banshees, management and workers. Six years ago, they were down to half that. And then last winter we lost more, a lot of the city children and a huge number of banshees besides, after one of us got bit on a mission, said nothing, came home and turned. A devastation. Weeks of culling, the infected and the healthy. Our fighting numbers may never recover. Death outside the walls and death within.

There are rumours of illness again down in the shanties, of bad water spreading, of bodies heaved over the walls in the darkness of night. A wariness in the banshee buildings. Looking at these faces, I believe it. Things are getting worse here. The city is failing. When I arrived, six long years ago, things were already bad. My relief at finding people, at finding people like me, who moved like I did, it lasted till our first mission.

I breathe. Thinking too much.

I can see now for sure that it's B-Troop bringing in this person who'll be punished. I squint against the light, catch the troop leader just as she gives an almighty whack with an elbow, making the wretch stumble. I look away, my chest feeling tight.

Ash is working her way down the lined road ahead of the group, with the weight of respect banshees – the whole city, as far as I know – have for her, making the punishment likewise respectable. Directing her troops, tall and beautiful, so high-ranking now she's management really, in charge of all of us who dwell in her house, nearly all the banshees in the city, except those Guards. The Guards we do not get along with. This is partly because they think they're more skilled than us and partly because we think they might be right. Brutal, experienced, absolutely silent. Another few years, and Sene and Mare might be amongst them.

The group makes their progression through the crowds, the small figure with the hood and the banshees around her, pushing through the long, long line. There's not noise, exactly, but a sense of excitement and movement. My eyes are pulled back again and again to the little mob.

There are two to be punished today, being swept along by B-Troop. I never knew they'd do this to more than one person at a time. The worst thing you ever saw, now twice as bad. This Boyle must be something, even by management standards.

I get a sense of the desperates pushing up to get a look, to get a go. They're so beat down, there's nowhere for their anger to go only out. There's a madness that sets on the city when we gather like this. There's a feeling these scrawns could be capable of anything.

My heart rate has been going up steadily and now

my hands start to vibrate. I breathe out, close my eyes, breathe out again. I keep thinking up ways to try and do something different here, and I can't get any that make sense.

The three thousand-odd souls won't all be here. There're sick, old and young, those on duty. Those who just don't want to see it, though a troop or two of banshees will have been sent round to gather them up. Last time that duty was ours too; this time word came from Ash to stand with management.

I don't want to see it.

The crowd is getting pushy. There's little noise still, but I see jostling and fists. These aren't the kinds of disturbances we're meant to pay attention to.

I look for Agata and find her, standing at the bottom of the steps, her face stern and blank. Even so, I draw comfort from her. And I'm glad for these two who are to be punished that they are blindfolded. I've lived here six years now and this is nearly too much for me, so it is: the noise of them, the faces, each one different. I want to turn on my heel and run smartly back to banshee quarters, get in my hammock, turn my face towards the cool wall and close my eyes.

Even better to run *home* home, all those clicks west again, get to my island, stomp up the stairs, slam my bedroom door. For a moment I can smell the cool salty freshness, the clean linen. The riches we had. I close my eyes, breathe out the salt air of home. More real than what's happening in front of me. Ash and B-Troop are near now, and when I look at our House Mother I think she's staring back at me till I realise she's looking at Boyle. I glance behind and he's returning her look, his eyes narrowed, his face satisfied. I look away before they see me watching.

My eyes fall on senior management standing at the bottom of the second set of steps. Puffed out, clean faces, heavy breathing, hair.

There's a sudden hush, even in the quiet, and I realise that, behind and above me, Boyle has stepped forward and raised his hands. Whatever little noise the crowd makes is hushed. They love to hear management talk, so they do, and there's the same excitement when a new leader steps forward, usually over the body of the last. They've been coming more quickly these last years. A sign of desperation, Agata says. As if he – always he – will herald change for the better.

'We,' he says. His voice crackles and booms; there is absolute quiet. Imagine having the power to shout to the whole city in this way, demanding we come to listen. Insisting we meanwhile keep quiet.

'We are the last!' He shouts it, one word at a time. I am just close enough to see the pinkening of his skin with the effort, the veins rising on his throat. I look out to the crowd and see thousands of faces turned up towards us. Men and women and children. Arms in the air – an acceptably silent show of approval for management.

'On this, a day of unity, we remember. We are the last ones left. Phoenix City is the only safety, our refuge. Our home! To run from it is to run from us; to run from us is to run from life.'

There's truth to what he's saying, that's the power of it. There is nobody else out there, no other cities or strongholds. The banshees, back when there were more of them, walked the length and breadth of the country. I'm the last one they found out there.

'The skrake came and the world fell. But Phoenix City still stands!'

I can nearly feel the beat of the skrake outside our walls. They are just metres away, pressing in, excited by the noise and the smell of us all together. We're leaning out on one side, the skrake leaning in on the other. All of us looking for blood.

'Life here is sacred,' Boyle says, and the city blinks up at him.

So sacred they'll kill you for trying to live it the way you want to.

Boyle's silence goes on for longer than I'd have thought

possible. Don't we all feel the same thing, the meaty pulse of fingers the other side of the wall stretching out for our flesh? All this racket, all these bodies gathered in one handy place. For a moment I feel so thoroughly the push of the skrake that the great sweaty stink of the city seems delicious.

There's movement just behind me and then a hand on my shoulder. I startle so fully that my feet nearly leave the ground. There's a titter of near-silent laughter. I look at the hand, follow the arm to a stern management face: one of Boyle's men. He tugs at me and when I glance at our leader, he's gesturing to me impatiently. I step a little unsteadily to stand beside him, aware of the thousands of eyes, feeling absolutely separate from them and the city and even my own body.

What am I *doing* here?

Boyle does not look at me but he grasps my wrist roughly in his hot wet hand and lifts my arm towards the sky with his own. I get a whiff of him: darkly sweet. As he raises his arm I can't help but picture his sweaty armpit, drenched hair tufting out of it.

'Proof!' he shouts. 'She did not grow up inside the safety of the city walls! But as soon as she could walk she made her way here. To safety.'

I grew up safe, I think, doing justice to my mothers in my head at least. I was the safest child in Ireland. They kept me on the island from skrake, and away from all of this. They died, and I couldn't bear the silence, so I went looking for people and I found them, on the road to the city: Cillian, Nic and little Aodh.

I have to whisper the truth to myself occasionally, I'm finding. They'll take it off you if you're not careful.

They were running from the city, from the banshees, and those banshees picked me up instead. I was dragged here, though I was willing, blindfolded and bound. My banshees.

'The city provides! The city saves!' Boyle is shouting, and the crowd raises their own arms, mimicking ours.

'Say it,' Boyle says quietly to me. He lets my arm drop but does not look at me. He hasn't once looked at me.

I don't know exactly what he wants me to say, but I open my mouth anyway. If I think too much about speaking in front of this great crowd a part of me will come to a stop, just like before.

'There is nothing out there,' I shout, unthinking, almost eager. 'Only death!' My voice is a little rough from lack of use and I'm surprised at the sound of myself; my shout higher than I remember. My face is hot and my throat burns. I'd have shouted anything at all to let him be done with me but, still, Boyle will not leave go of my hand.

'To leave is to die!' Boyle shouts; my ears ring. 'And we give those who wish to leave their will!'

The speaking part is over. Out in the crowd, hands are lowered, or brought over their eyes so they can better see against the sun.

The bound figures, surrounded by banshees, are pressed forward through the crowds for the last part of the ordeal, and I'm let go. Boyle's men close around him once more, those who bothered standing in the first place, and the dozen Guards around them.

I'm being touched again and though it's not such a surprise this time, nobody laughs at my flinch, and Boyle says, his face impassive, his voice calm, his eyes elsewhere: 'You will go to the end of the plinth with them.' I feel for a moment as if I've swallowed something jagged. I can only look at him.

The duty kept for Guards, usually, to walk the punished to the end of the plinth. To see them off it, whatever is left of them, to push them if necessary, down to the straining black jaws of the skrake.

'Rewards for loyalty are great.'

This new horror is meant as a show of favour.

I put one foot in front of the other to take up my new place at the slimmer end of the plinth. I breathe in and I breathe out and I keep my eyes on my feet, one moving steadily past the other, propelling me forwards as if I am being carried by something outside of my own control.

Which I am.

Which is what we all tell ourselves. Which is what the city runs on, after all.

I do what I'm told. I stand near the leader at the base of the plinth, waiting to finish murdering these women. This is how I help the cause for justice in this city.

Empathy is the weapon he's using against us. Drawing it out so he can kill it dead. Whatever's left.

One of the women can hardly walk. Now they're let be together, one clutches at the other, helping her up, holding her tight. Some of the pieces of filth that the people below have saved to use, or picked up off the rubbish heaps, have been left in them: smashed sharp bits of plastic are left deep in the skin, sometimes only the very ends poking out.

My heart.

The banshees propel the two women on. There is something about that one leg working forwards that seems to me utterly heroic.

I can feel my throat begin to burn again. I wish now for time to go backwards instead of forwards. I look away, forwards, anywhere, blinking quickly.

The banshees get the wretches up the steps to our plinth. They manhandle the two women, one nearly doubled over, towards Boyle. Two Guards get behind them while he straightens and looks out to the crowd. He does not need to wait for their attention. A knife is put into his hand and he holds it up, pauses a moment, and then thrusts it, with more force than I would have thought him capable of and no hesitation at all, into the belly of one of the women: she doesn't make a noise but the other screams. Her arms are held tight behind her while she goes on screaming and Boyle stabs her too, a big meaty arm shaking with the effort of it. The second woman closes in on the wound with a sigh.

They loved each other, these women.

I cannot keep my eyes off them now. I will not do them the injustice of looking away. One of them has a part of her scalp showing, the hair has been torn out so viciously. I can see their sweat, the smeared blood on skin. The one with the leg, her skin is beautifully smooth, like Agata's skin. They are both living beings still. Can we not help even now? Can we not save them? I want to say that I love them both, someone loves them and they're doing well. I'm glad they've each other up here at the end to cling on to, but for them that'll be the greatest agony.

As I watch, the woman with the leg struggles to stand straighter. Holding one of her arms close to her with the other, she raises her eyes to Boyle. Her lips move – and then she spits. She tries to. I am certain of it. She goes to move towards him but she is too slow, too wounded. The Guard stops her almost casually.

I glance at Boyle and see that he is pleased. He looks at one of his banshees for just a moment, but there is approval in his face – his features changing from disgust to a righteous complacency. A problem has been resolved; control is regained, publicly, and the world is as it should be. He has thrust his precious knife into two women and now, moments later, he is thinking about something else entirely. He straightens, then tilts his head – a message to me to do my part now.

I've seen other favoured Guards perform this duty so I know that it is my role now to walk with the two women to the end of the plinth, to the part hanging over the city walls. The two Guards with them move to help them. Without thinking, I hold up a hand to them and they stop and stay where they are.

They both find it difficult to move and difficult to breathe. I can hear gasps of air coming and going, ragged and wheezing. They're both limping badly now, one with her leg and the other with the knife still in her belly.

Ahead of me, clinging to each other, they make their way slowly towards the end of the plinth, hanging over the city walls.

'It is nearly over,' I whisper. I think I started saying it to try and comfort them but the words are carried away. Even if the two women could hear the words they're beyond me now; the city has pushed them off beyond us all.

The tapered end of the plinth, the part that leans over the wall, has room for the two of them – just. We move forwards together, inch by inch, till the three of us stand on the edge.

The women have turned to look at each other. They cling to each other, foreheads together but eyes open. One lets out a long, shaky sob and the other puts her bleeding hand gently to her cheek. We spend an eternity up here, the two women breathing their last in time with each other, bleeding.

'Are you ready?' I ask, because to break the silence is awful but less awful than what I will do next.

I cannot help looking down. We are beyond the wall now. Beneath us the skrake crush together; dead eyes and rotten skulls and fingers and proboscises all reach up.

The banshee with the knife in her gut tries once more to straighten. Her lips curl back in agony over her teeth. With a great cry she puts both hands to the handle of the knife in her gut. She pulls till it comes, hissing out a sour breath with it.

As I watch she brings the knife up, quicker than my tired eyes, and stabs her friend in the neck – the blade has slid in and out quicker than it takes to blink. The woman sighs and her eyes begin to close. The woman with the knife holds her close once more, shutting her eyes tight, whispering something in her ear, and then, smoothly, throws her over the edge.

She turns to me.

She holds the handle of the knife out to me with shaking bloody hands. Her fingers long and beautiful, her poor livid blood.

Her eyes meet mine. 'Use it,' she hisses. I reach out to her as she steps back off the plinth to the ravening horde below us, thinking she wants me to take her, to finish things for her before she falls to the skrake. Her hand reaches up towards mine as she falls and I understand her.

For a moment our fingers touch.

House Mother

I N THE AFTERNOONS WE TRAIN TOGETHER IN THE square.

No matter what's going on in the city or what's going on between us, or with other banshees, or . . . no matter what, the way we fight together is the same.

Today we're pitted against D-Troop, who're trying to break in two new ones. Takes a while for the greens to come good, and D-Troop are historically weak banshees, shy, hesitant in the field. There's a lot of working together with greenuns, trying to make things fit. The elder ones try to make space for the new ones, try to show them how it's done.

We fight to get good at fighting, but it's about bonding

as well, and here I am, still, bonded. We'll never know anyone the way we know each other.

D-Troop are playing dirty. One of the team, one of the newbies, has a little bar of something up her arm guard and it hits like a bitch. If she'd been around longer she'd know better. It's up to us to teach her.

Agata manoeuvres across the square so she's facing up to her. Even two years ago she'd have had to wink at me first but now I know. I know the reasons behind every step, every breath she takes. Agata takes the hit, invites a big left from the newbie, goes down harder than she strictly needs to. The newbie hesitates – she only wanted to keep up – but just as she begins to suspect there might be trouble I smash into her like a rock, vaulting off Agata's back, supering my fist straight into her nose.

It crunches and down she goes. I hold out my hand to Agata and once she's up we look over the newbie together. Blood streaming. She'll be all right. Agata relents first, helping her up, and then I join her. Agata purses her lips and I try not to smile.

Following some instinct, I glance behind me, and there's Ash, watching, laughing silently. She gets up, comes towards us – towards me. She raises an eyebrow, like, 'Nice trick,' and I smile and let my eyes drop to say thank you. She squares up to me and my heart starts going mad. I try to play up to it as I sense the other banshees making a ring around us, everyone coming in for a look. It's not often Ash gets up to try out one of us. I'll play up to it, make a big show of being bashful, then come roaring at her with my fists – but that in itself is a feint, and I'm trying to get the legs out from under her. It works, more or less, but she flips up and comes for me. I get in a few punches, something lands nicely, but then I feel a great crack on my head and for a moment I wonder if the sky has fallen.

I'm on my back in the dirt. Ash stands above me, the sun haloing her proud head, smiling with big white teeth and offering her hand.

We can say nothing under the sky, but that night, at dinner, the banshees are merciless.

Deep in the bowels of banshee quarters, the bottom of the basement, where we eat in shifts. Where, sometimes, we can talk. They talk. I stay quiet and take it.

'Are you sure you want to eat with us?'

'Yeah, won't Ash and Boyle want you?'

'Ugh, Lin, perverse,' Agata winces, and the others titter.

I spoon warm mash into myself and take a deep draught of the boiled water, catching Mare and Sene exchange a look. I don't know what it means.

Anyway, Ash is one thing. Boyle is another. It pinches.

I want to remind them that I didn't want to go up there: I didn't want to look into the eyes of that woman as she fell. They know these things already. They're not trying to sting, they're trying to take the sting *out*. I finger the knife that dying woman gave me, stowed carefully in my shin guard, and as I reach down I feel Agata's fingers in mine. A brief squeeze. I glance up and her face is soft.

We know, her eyes say.

They do, really. Aoife and Lin do, anyway.

'We're a team,' Mare says just then, maybe reading my mind.

'Us against the skrake,' we respond in unison, Lin rolling her eyes outright.

Truth is, we rarely fight skrake. Mostly we fight each other.

Night.

I'm woken in the dark with a rough hand. It takes me a minute to come to. I was somewhere deep, somewhere far from here.

I push my legs out over the edge of the hammock into the cold. It's Aoife's snores that remind me where I am, more, even, than the smell of the place. I love that, even while she's forced to be quiet, noise finds a way out of her.

The runner's arm is insistent.

There's no point asking the kid where we're going so I don't, but we're heading upstairs. I glance at Agata's sleeping huddle behind me.

Even I know we must be going to Ash's rooms. Eight long sets of steep steps, worn slippy. The banisters are gone, used for firewood two winters ago.

Like most house heads, Ash lives in a comfortable apartment at the top of the building. The corridors coming off the staircases are long and dark. I can't even see to the end of them. I can hear murmurs; I sense people all around us, but the building up here feels empty all the same.

We come to her door. There's light on the other side of it, a sudden brightness after all the dark. A heavy curtain (the *expense* of the fabric – you could clothe three people in the shanties with it) is held aside for me and I step into a large room. It is long if not tall, warm with a comfortable little fire blazing in a hearth. My skin prickles as if each part of it wants to reach out towards the heat. There are *candles*. There are books everywhere, on shelves, on little tables. I stare. There're *rugs*.

Ash is stirring from a couch in front of the fire, putting her book down, moving gracefully to come and meet us. She's fluid and her shape is rounded, not ragged and hard like mine. Her height seems particularly powerful somehow in these rooms. There's more to her: she's substantial, filled out and generous looking. She looks well fed; she looks like life has been easy for her, easy and pleasant. I suppose I know that it hasn't been. She looks like she's from a different world altogether than the rest of us. Being in the same room with her is something else. I feel shabby, small and sharp beside her.

Whether it's the warmth of the fire or the climb or fatigue, but I blink and the ground has come up and grabbed me.

'Liv,' Ash is saying. I am still blinking stupidly, trying to put it all together: why I am lying on the floor.

I try to get up but the woman puts her hand on my chest and even in my fug of confusion I can feel the power in it.

'Stay down, give yourself a minute.'

Did I lose a track of time somehow? Have I been transported? I close my eyes and I breathe out. The world slowly comes right. I have fainted before. She leans over me, her face lined but soft, oddly colourful; pale skin, paler than mine, but such red lips, such blue eyes.

There are red spots in my vision.

'You're not fed much below,' the woman is saying to me gently, as if the rations the kitchens dole out are nothing to do with her. Maybe they aren't.

Carefully, slowly, she reaches out one long-fingered

hand and brushes hair back from my forehead. A gentle, mothering sort of touch. I close my eyes and it's suddenly hard for me not to cry. I shrink away, I struggle up.

'Hello, Orpen,' she says, her deep voice soft, like a rich fabric. 'You fainted,' she says, and I flush. 'It's a miracle you made it up the stairs, really. Are you hungry?'

I shake my head, blinking.

'You'll feel better if you eat a little. Trust me.'

There's something so appealing about the gentle way she says it that I nod and when she gives me her hand I reach out and take it and she helps me to my feet. The world blinks in and out of focus again and my legs are a little bit weak but I'm OK.

She doesn't leave go of my hand and she guides me over to the other side of the fireplace, to a chair set half in the shadows.

I hear another set of footsteps and tense, but it's Liv again, with a plate and a cup to set on a small table beside me.

'Thanks,' Ash tells her, and Liv nods, then turns and leaves the room without so much as a backwards glance. I want her to look back at me, I want her to tell me with her eyes that this is OK, that this is normal.

I feel very foolish.

I wish I wasn't so filthy.

'It's OK,' Ash tells me, like she's peered right into my head, and I am so surprised that I look straight back at her.

'Eat,' she says, gesturing to the plate with one elegant hand.

I'll have to mind my thoughts around her, somehow, if I'm to be around her. She talks to troop leaders, usually, not the likes of me – especially not me, an outlier. How does Mare manage it, I wonder.

'Eat,' Ash says again, and she withdraws a little.

I move my hand to the first thing it finds on the plate in front of me and I bring it to my lips and let my eyes wander around the room, getting used to the gloom of the corners, back to the shelves of books. Ash sinks down on to her couch and takes up some knitting and pretends to ignore me, for which I'm grateful.

My appetite is rising now that I've swallowed a few bites and I look back to my plate. A lozenge of white: chicken. Chicken with salt. My mouth floods wet and I put it to my lips and swallow it down, and my stomach gurgles in excitement. I'm mortified, but I chew and swallow and take a big gulp from the cup – water, cold, soft as rainwater. Delicious.

'You knit?' Ash asks quietly, not stopping what she's doing. I watch her add a thread, click by click, with some magic of her hands to a line, making a garment.

I shake my head again.

'It's hard to find anything to knit with,' she says. 'But then, my banshees bring me back what they can.'

It's true, we do bring her back what we can, tuck it away.

Her eyes flash to mine.

'Our little secret,' she says, and she blinks just one eye and then looks back to her hands before I can react.

We sit in silence and I finish what's on my plate. I lick my lips and look about me again, my eyes lingering on the books.

'You read?'

I nod.

'They used to teach that to everyone here in the city . . . our House Mother taught us when I was growing up. Then new orders came in. New leadership. You know how it is.' She glances over at me and our eyes meet again. I feel something like a flush come across me, like she trusts me, like I've earned that. 'I can loan you something.' She pauses and then smiles at me, a big, warm smile, looking down at her hands again, to the clacking of her knitting.

'You were honoured today.'

I'm not going to tell her it didn't feel like honour, so I stay quiet.

'And what did you make of Boyle?'

I can only stare. Am I meant to have opinions about management, as if it were something I could ever affect?

She makes a sort of closed up shape with her lips. 'He and I have known each other for a long time.'

The relief of having kept my mouth shut. I blink and take another gulp of water, feel it go cool and clean down my gullet.

'He's going to make a difference here.'

I want to ask which problems he'll deal with first and how, but can't trust myself to say anything that won't sound aggressive.

Ash looks at me under her eyelashes and smiles. 'Cracking down on city violence.' We do more violence than anyone in this city, I know well. 'There's even talk he'll promote women to higher positions.'

I've nothing to say to that either. What does it matter whether it's men or women ordering the violence?

Ash seems to take my silence as a kind of enthusiasm and I'm disappointed. I thought she might know me a little better than that. 'Well, I'm glad you and I are friends. He's right, the city needs someone of your . . . talent. You could go far, you know.' She gestures around her a little. 'Set up a nice life for yourself, if you're obedient, if you show us how useful you can be.'

'Those two women,' I say. 'The ones punished.'

Ash looks at me sharply. I didn't know that I was

going to ask about them, only that my hand has not felt the same since that woman touched it. Only that I have not stopped thinking about them and I don't think I ever will.

'Yes?'

'Who were they?'

'Just women,' Ash says, taking her time with her words, but not like she has trouble picking them. A little sadness comes across her handsome face. 'It doesn't matter terribly – they obviously were not doing their part.' She smiles again. 'I forget that you do not all know each other. It wasn't always so.'

'They're good at keeping us apart,' I say, and then wish that I hadn't. I feel that I'm giving myself away. I remember the feeling of the dying banshee's fingers on mine as she fell. 'What did they do?'

Ash gives me a long look.

'It seems harsh, I know. Perhaps it is.' Her face hardens a little and I know I've pressed too far already. 'The world is harsh.'

'What's left of it,' I say.

Ash lets out a sighing laugh and nods. 'But, there was a problem – perhaps you've seen the men around the city, hobbled?'

I shake my head.

'Management solves problems,' Ash smiles. 'That's

what we do, too. I supported Boyle and now he'll support us,' she smiles. 'Understand?'

I'm not sure what she's asking me, but I nod.

'Good girl,' Ash smiles. 'Mare and Sene being good to you?' she asks then, the corner of one mouth lifting just a little, her head held just a shade to one side.

'Of course,' I say, surprised.

Ash looks away, nods thoughtfully.

'Liv?' she says. In a flash the girl is back with us, leaning towards Ash in her need to listen and obey. 'Send up Mare, will you?' The girl nods and disappears. 'There's a mission for your team, straight from Boyle. Mare will tell you more about it, I'm sure.' She smiles a dazzling smile and I feel that we've a secret between us.

I smile back at her again. The conversation is over. Whatever she wanted to say to me is said. I want to stay here, to be favoured by her, to be warm and safe with her. I want to be taken care of.

As I get up to go out into the cold once more, she reaches out and takes my hand. Her skin is soft and clean and I inhale deeply. 'Management like you,' she smiles. 'And as we know, management are always right.'

I think she is joking with me. Her face is very close to mine.

'You could do very well.'

Mission

OUR MISSION IS A SQUIB AND IT LOOKS LIKE WE'LL BE headed home again to disappoint our masters.

I don't know whether any of us are letting ourselves think on it this moment. We don't talk about that, or our worry that there's a greenun out with us, or the murder of the two banshees at Boyle's inaugural punishment. Even when we're out and can talk, we don't really *talk*, not about the important things, not when we're close to the city.

There's chat, though. This moment we are at Aoife for her taste. She's well used it.

'Big donkey nose on him,' Sene says, too poised and serious ever to smile but letting warmth into her voice.

'And the hair!' Agata beside me, her voice light on the air. She glances over at me to see am I laughing too.

'Could be a breeder with hair like that,' Sene says.

'Aye, he's pretty,' Lin says.

'But his nose!' Sene can never let the nose go.

'It was broke. That's not his fault.'

'What does he do, himself and his nose?' Agata asks.

Aoife is quiet for a moment and then allows: 'He's a waller.'

Jeers all round. I join in, even, laughing, though never leaving my eyes off the country around us. I feel surprised and I think about why this is. Wallers are held in low regard in the city. Doing back-breaking work for barely enough to live on, selling the strength of their bodies. As if that isn't what we all do, in one direction or another. At least wallers do some actual protecting, is what I'm beginning to think.

'Nothing wrong with being a waller,' Mare says quietly, and the laughs die down. I know she's right, but having someone to joke about, having someone we can feel superior to, even in our own misery, it helps us. Management encourages it.

I glance back and am relieved to see little Jay, the greenun out with us, doesn't seem to be listening, or understanding. You cannot be too careful, even with the small ones. There're reprisals for banshees showing any hints of sexual agency. *Any* agency, but the sexual really seems to get them on edge.

It is so good to be out, to be stretching out in the fresh air, to be let speak. Even if we may be going home empty-handed. People will die, but sure, don't they always?

We've swept within a ten-click arc of the city. Even I know there's nothing left. We make a desultory search through the flat grey landscape. On the outskirts of the city where the buildings aren't so dangerous and the skrake fewer, we pick again through broken glass and too-tall weeds. We see the marks of the banshees that came before us: there was nothing for those women to gather and bring home, or the ones who came before them.

The city needs everything. Clothes or cloth of any type; oil; pots and containers. We'd be heroes if we found tins; we'd be lauded if ever we found seeds. I'd give a finger for a toothbrush in its wrapping, a tooth for a bar of soap. I've got places I'd put those things to sneak them into the city.

I know where there are some of these things. In a cupboard in a kitchen on an island far away, on the other side of the country.

Perhaps they are being used now, by the runaways. Cillian, Nic and Aodh. I still think of Nic as being pregnant, but that child, if she lives, will be six now. Little Aodh will be about the age of this greenun we have with us, Jay. I glance at her, her fresh, placid, hopeful face, intent on keeping up with us. Not knowing enough to know we should not be looked up to.

We keep our ears tightly trained on the world around us, and not just for skrake. Rations are short, even on missions, and if we can kill an animal, so much the better for us. Precious wildlife left.

There's a low whistle from the rear of the troop and Mare hangs back to investigate while the four of us move on. Agata walks on a step or two and I slow till I'm walking with Aoife.

'How does he feel about your love?' I ask quietly into the back and forth about her waller, and as soon as I do I regret it. I know that's not what this conversation was about. The silence that follows on makes me blush. I still don't know how to be normal with others. I'll always be weird, even amongst my own.

Difference is good, Agata has told me, but she stays quiet now and the silence lengthens, and I feel my cheeks warm.

I glance towards the back of the troop and see Sene stepping in with Jay.

This is how it's done; you're a child but you want to be a banshee. You've taken a look at being a breeder maybe, and you decide there's less blood and pain this way. You might be right. I've heard the screams coming from their part of the city when I'm out on patrol.

You train with us, best you can, and you come out on a few missions with us to get a feel for it, and if you don't die and the training has gone OK you get shadowed by a more experienced banshee. It was good luck they didn't kill me, but they could see I'd been trained, and there's a respect among banshees. Agata protected me and she's respected, by Sene and Mare, maybe, especially. I came looking for them. There was that, too.

She's just a girl, this Jay. They're sounding out a lot of girls on missions now, trying to bulk up our numbers, get more banshees working. Looking at her, you'd have to think she's too young to be out in a dangerous world. We like her, though. There's a good energy off her. Nice to have Sene and Mare occupied with her a bit as well. There's shame amongst banshees in losing a young one out on a mission so we're all keeping an eye on her. Our team, we – they – lost three banshees a long time ago, Agata's mate and two others besides on some botched mission. They never talk about their lost friends and I do not ask. Still, we're down in our numbers and the only reason more haven't been foisted on us is because Mare and Sene want it that way, and have some sway with Ash.

'We meet,' Aoife says at last, kindly, and I feel a surge of gratitude towards her.

'And he feels the way you feel?'

She shrugs, pink blooming into her pale skin.

'Whisht,' Agata says, her eyes glancing towards the back of the troop. Aoife isn't meant to have feelings for anybody; she's not to be meeting anybody. How she manages it at all is wild to me.

Even amongst banshees we've to be careful. There are rewards to be had for turning against each other in Phoenix City.

I wonder would Mare report it. But if it wasn't for Mare we wouldn't be let out on missions at all. Mare, tall, dark skin smooth over high cheekbones and broad shoulders, short hair so grey it is nearly white. A cruel cold look to her face, though she is not as mean-looking as Sene, her second-in-command.

We're really moving, I notice. Teasing Aoife is nearly an excuse to not notice how focused we are. There's a skittishness amongst us, an objective we don't know but we're trusting anyway, and I'm only realising it now.

Agata glances round at me again and I meet her eye. At the back of the troop Mare still walks with Jay. I must make sure to keep an eye on the child when Mare is called away, and even as the thought sparks through me

I see she gets a nod from Sene, now working her way back up the troop.

I break formation away from Aoife to bring up the rear, Agata coming back with me. Jay (Aodh, my heart says) is so tender it's nearly hard to look at her. Her fresh skin and big hopeful eyes and light step. Her hair too long for a real banshee, a kid's hair still. Whatever plan is going on here – if there is a plan – I don't know if Jay's part of it or might be a hindrance. That's a worry as well, so it is. Mare and Sene keep up the pace. There's a plan.

'Nice to be out of them city walls, hah?' Agata says lightly.

'Yes,' Jay says, breathless. Mare; Agata. Me especially. All legends in the tiny banshee community. She's so happy to be here. She feels totally safe.

'You're not frightened?'

We walk three or four steps while Jay tries to think of the best thing to say to this.

Lin glances back at us from her place next up the line and says seriously, 'I am. We've never been up this far north, not on a day trip.'

I don't know whether this is meant to scare the child or if it's true. It's uncomfortable for me to have so many similarities to this child after years as part of the troop. I'm easily led, too. Despite all the years, I still feel ignorant. This twelve-year-old knows more about the outskirts of the city than I do.

What I do know is that if we're taking out a greenun we never stay overnight. Since we lost a whole troop – six strong women, experienced banshees, never heard from again – day missions is all we get, and sometimes even with management tagging along, making pricks of themselves. Management measures are only good for the laugh, as Aoife says.

'I'm not frightened,' the girl says to Agata, in a steady voice, though quiet.

'We're not on a day trip,' Mare says.

The silence is tense afterwards for a long time.

We've been coming north, a stony walk along very old tracks, moving steady through the overgrowth. We pause outside a tunnel dug through the hills, but nothing except us moves through the darkness, even if it smells of death and shit.

Blinking into the light on the other side, Mare and Sene pick up the pace again, but at this stage the sun is high in the sky and even I know if we want to be sure of making it back in one day we'll have to turn now and bear through that tunnel again. I glance at Agata and every time I look at her I know more thoroughly that something's on.

There's something about the day, about the freshness

of the breeze, of being outside the city. As free as it gets. Maybe it is this, or maybe it is the knife given me that makes me want to act out, to make an impression on the world again.

'Now, Greenun,' Aoife is saying. 'Let me tell you the story of how the banshees came to be.'

We all groan – we've heard this many times – but Jay smiles and moves closer to her.

'A long time ago, before there were skrake,' Aoife begins, 'men were the most dangerous physical threat to women.'

You live your life in the city, that hasn't changed, I think, and then I think, actually, banshees are the threat now.

'Why are there always two of us?' the girl asks.

'So they can always drag us apart again,' Lin says. 'So they'll always have something on us.'

'In the old days they'd say that if women walked in twos, they wouldn't be attacked,' Aoife speaks over her. 'It was safer that way.'

'But why?' asks Jay, her face furrowed.

'Two women are usually stronger than one man,' Aoife says. 'And now we're trained, we're much stronger.'

'But why—'

'It's just the way the way it is,' Mare says shortly, looking at the girl and then back to Aoife, eyes blazing.

I hate her, I think. I hate her for not leading us the way I want to be led. I think I started hating her when she beat me to shit on the road six years ago, though it's only now, outside the walls with space to think, with a dead woman's knife in my hand, that I can put language to the feeling.

We pick up the pace. Quiet and deadly, we meet nothing on our way. There's a theory that the belt around Dublin is nearly empty of skrake because they've all been attracted to the city within it. Every skrake within a ten-click radius of Phoenix City has heard us or smelled us and is trying to get in, pushing hard against our walls.

On our right is the sea, and in places the tracks go just alongside it. It's beautiful, moving under a green glaze like muscles under smooth skin. We glimpse little beaches. We could make our way down and pull off our clothes and get good and clean, but Mare wouldn't hear of it and we wouldn't ask her, most of us. If you're outside the city walls, you're ready for battle and that's a rule.

I wonder what'd happen if we just upped and killed Mare.

We'd have to kill Sene too, probably, which would be hard; two of the toughest banshees around. But I think then we could stay out, Agata and me. Aoife and Lin too, who I love. We could bathe in the sea, pick which direction to go next. We could *survive*, go west. Together.

Me and Agata. This is what I want, I think, if I had to name it. Freedom, but not alone.

And I know that we wouldn't be happy, not for long, not with just the two of us or even four of us. People need more. But, it's nice to think about that cool sea on our warm skins.

'You're the outlier,' Jay is saying next to me, and I give her a look. I'll never not be an outlier. She is only curious, but I do not answer questions, not if I can help it.

Here they come, still and all.

'How did you live?' she asks, so quiet I can barely hear her above the noise of the breeze moving through the trees. I've made this mistake before, being drawn to the newest banshees, wanting to keep an eye out for them. I'm looking for something in her, I know that. We're all like this with the fresh faces coming up, like breeders around a baby.

I want to hear what the troop tell the greenuns, about our rules, about this world, in case I learn something. Instead, here's what happens: they know who I am and they've questions I can't answer. I roll my head on my neck and ignore her.

I drop behind a little to bring up the rear, use the opportunity to give a good stretch and look about me, and while I do I see a light drop of red half-run down the kid's leg. I wait for Agata to glance my way and then nod towards the issue. Her lips draw back tight over her teeth. It is a problem. We're not meant to leave the city walls if we're bleeding. Agata drops back to walk beside me and lets her head fall next to mine.

'Poor kid, she probably hasn't felt it yet.'

'Should we escort her back?' That's what management would have us do.

Sometimes Agata doesn't bother to respond when she knows I know the answer already.

'This is going to be an overnighter, isn't it?'

A little fear has crept into my whisper, which I don't feel good about. Whatever Mare is planning, we won't get back before dark. I don't know how she squared it with management. The thought of spending a night out with a fresh, menstruating girl . . . Six of us, only.

'It's probably not even true that skrake can smell them,' Agata says. 'Management don't know what they're talking about.'

Agata thinks management are afraid of women. She thinks they like to keep us walled up when we're menstruating because they're frightened of it. Lin says she only wishes they were afraid of us.

The wind changes and I'm overwhelmed by a sudden and shocking sense of home: the constant wind they'd call the *shinaun* on the island, and the sounds of the waves and the low voices of my family in the kitchen. The smell of seaweed.

The feeling comes so strong, but then vanishes, leaving me bereft.

When I first came to the city these flashes of the past would leave me breathless, on my knees in the dirt. They come less often now and I've learned to treat them like a few last tired press-ups. Breathe through, try to relax. It doesn't have to mean anything. There's a job ahead of us to do.

I know Agata is looking at me, but I keep my blurry eyes pointed straight ahead and on we go, and after a little while I can look over at her and wink. Are you all right, she was asking me, and me telling her yeah, good enough. I can keep going.

We've been walking a while now and the sun is aiming downwards. Mare leads us inland and nobody suggests we turn, or questions her or pauses, even. We're heading north. Lin was not wrong.

We've said nothing to Jay but someone else did, or she noticed herself, because the streak of blood along the soft pale flesh of her leg has been cleaned. Did she wipe it with something and then throw that thing away? Will she be doing that the whole way? I shake my head and let the thought away. Poor child must be in pain, apart from all this. She's cloud white but there's not a peep out of her. Her little legs working away as quick as they can.

Ahead of me the talk has turned to one of our favourite topics and that is other troops. Mare is close to our house mother, Ash. Word is, they came from the same breeder though I never heard that anyone was brave enough to ask this outright. They hold themselves apart, Mare and Sene.

Ash – bright, enduring, loyal to the city, beloved by the higher-ups, especially now, with Boyle installed as leader. Ash is too valuable to be let beyond the walls, or maybe she's no interest in that any more, so it's Mare's troop that's the preferred gang for any new mission. The city knowing me as the outlier seems to single out our troop for a special kind of attention. It's as though management like to think of me putting myself in danger for the good of the city.

The next troop, B-Troop, has been riding our heels for a long time now. They're fresher is their argument when their troop leader, Saoirse, goes to Ash looking for missions, but so far our experience, or Ash's love for Mare, has won out. If your troop gets out more, you can bring back more, and if you can bring back something useful enough, you'll buy your next outing.

There are so few missions now, with numbers down and troops disappearing. If we didn't get most of the missions going, we'd never leave the city walls. They don't let us go out far, but then they're disappointed we bring nothing back. With nothing brought back, they're worried again about losing their most senior hands when we're needed in the city. All this training for nothing, and no hope for everyone needing supplies back home.

I wonder how relieved I'd be, eventually, if we'd to stay in the city walls; stay quiet. It's OK once you're out here, but the walls begin to feel safe if you spend long enough behind them. You start to feel like you need them. You nearly forget there's a world outside. You forget how to make decisions.

'Where are we going?' I ask Agata under the cover of Aoife and Lin chatting about how best to go about a coddle, which, to be honest, we've heard a good few times before.

Instead of answering, Agata throws her eyes up and to the left and I follow them. There's a sign, mostly rusted away now, but with a picture still clear enough on it of something I can't make out, like a 't' or a cross nearly, but fatter.

'Airport.'

'Your reading is coming on,' I tell Agata, and she rewards me with a big smile, teeth white flashing against her brown skin. Hard not to grin back at a smile like that.

To get into the airport we've to hack our way through what's nearly a jungle. The land around the place is flat and lush with knotty growth. We work through it for a while and get Jay to hop up on Sene's broad shoulders so she can point us in the direction of the huge grey domes. Is there a smear of blood now on Sene's neck or is it just sweat? I try not to look.

In the heat of the afternoon we break to sit a while, drinking warm water from tired canteens and look about us.

'How'd you know about this place?' someone asks Mare, and I swear she glances at Agata before she answers.

'Found a map,' she says. 'Nobody's been out here in a long time. I don't know if anyone ever got inside.'

'This has been where we've been headed all this time?' I ask.

Mare nods. 'The Ring Road around the city is the safest way north.'

A few of us exchange glances – Lin's face is maybe even more serious looking than ever – and Aoife immediately starts talking about all the things she's going to find. 'And fuck me if I don't find new clothes, better wraps, some goddam *shoes* that fit right, a blade. Some food that doesn't taste like mother*fucking* ass . . .'

I catch Agata smiling and I feel the corners of my mouth lifting a little.

'You like ass, is what I heard,' I crack, mimicking the way they talk in the city.

I'm rewarded a big laugh and a look of admiration from the kid.

I love Aoife. Soon as she's out of the city her mouth opens up and she doesn't stop till we're back. She has so many thoughts all at once and ideally she wants to tell them all to us. It's refreshing. How many people like her are there in the city, I wonder, wanting to speak all the time and not being able. Women and men both. And the children.

You never know what's going on with people, is something I've learned these last years. Before that I'd always known exactly what was going on in a person's head, because I only knew my mothers growing up on a tiny wild island where everyone else was ate. That kind of knowledge is close to love, most of the time. I love Agata, but I don't cod myself that I always know what she's thinking. I trust her, though she's said nothing to me still about these disappearances of hers. She catches me looking at her and she smiles again. I trust her, whatever secrets she feels she needs to keep.

'Anybody see all these men hobbling around the city?' I ask. I didn't know I was going to ask it. Spent all these years pretty much silent and now my mouth keeps running away with me.

'Yeah,' Aoife says right away. 'All management guys?'

I nod. 'Management, being carried around by other people. Saw one out with two sticks under his arms.'

Nobody else says anything so Aoife starts up again. 'Strange, isn't it? Wonder what happened to them.'

'Let's keep moving,' Sene says.

'Have we orders?' Lin breaks through Aoife's rambling.

'Of course,' Mare says airily, but there's a stillness to her that makes us all pay attention. It is an odd response; it is not like her. Trying to speak like a feather when we all know she's a rock. And Sene a knife.

'Had we orders to come here and get something?' It's not like Lin to push so hard, though if anyone was going to push it'd be her, and I'm glad she's doing it. She and Agata and maybe Sene know what's going on. Leaving Lin and Aoife and me and the kid out of it. Agata should have told me, is how I feel about that.

Mare glances at Agata this time, so everyone knows she's in on it. 'It's no secret the city is out of just about everything we need. We've no cloth, we've no oil. It'll be good to look somewhere new.'

'C'mon, folks,' Agata says with a grin, after a moment. 'Management know what they're doing.'

Aoife guffaws and Lin smacks her on the shoulder and we get going.

Jay is pink, shocked, and I wonder again do we have to worry about her. The young ones are the most loyal to the city, is the way it goes. The ambitious ones rarely grow out of it. It's better to submit, most of the time. Even I can see that. Obey and keep the head down and give them what they want, and maybe they'll let you alone.

We come to a tall, barbed fence, intact, disappearing into the overgrowth as far as the eye can see to left and right. Sene gives us all the look and in a beat we're serious again. We take up defensive positions. She moves forward, rattles the thick wire, moves back again, crouching and prepped for whatever responds to the noise. We wait but nothing comes. Lin moves up then with her clippers and we cover her while she cuts, carefully and slowly, a gap big enough for us to fit through, two at a time, without cutting ourselves. I have never seen those clippers before and I know our kits backwards and forwards – we all do. Lin goes back to her position and then Mare gives the signal and we start moving forwards. Agata's face is pure work, pure focus. She doesn't meet my eye.

We don't love where we are. The grass is high and we've no sightlines through it. The wind rustling through it means we can hear nothing coming for us. The strange, cloudy buildings of the airport loom ahead of us till they tower, steel and glass shaped into curves, the sun glinting off its domes despite the years of dirt. Every now and then we'll come across some rusted barricade, the defences pointed outwards, towards us and towards the city. Abandoned or overrun in the Emergency.

'It's not a good position,' I can hear little Jay whisper behind me.

The way you hear about the outside from the city, the way they train you in there, it's all good elevations and no noise. I give her a look to quiet her. Her little face is pinched now as well as pale; frightened, though she's holding on tight. I give her a little smile, despite myself.

What we have found is that if there's no way into a building, there's a good chance nothing's been taken from it. There's also a chance there's skrake inside, stuck there from after the Emergency.

We keep as quiet as we can till we find a place we like, right between two huge oblongs of glass with clear sky between them, like a woman's parted legs. The purple concrete all round here is so thick the grass hasn't grown through it, and we at least get to look around us and breathe.

There's a hill we can get up so we've a bit of elevation

at least, but there's plenty of places to hide out here, in the overgrowth, behind the buildings.

We get into position.

First, we shout out. We've been making enough noise already, but seeing can we attract any skrake lurking about before they can surprise us is standard. Yelling out a battle cry feels awkward for a moment and then it feels good and natural. It feels powerful.

Movement, through the grass, coming towards us, fast.

'Form up,' Mare says, but we're already tightening. Agata is beside me and we face where the movements are coming from together, stance low, ready, weapons out, guards checked. Others are checking our rear. Mare is looking over us all, watchful, thinking of attacks, of defences.

I check for Jay and she's good; we've a protective circle around her. Even from where I stand I can see her shake, but her stance is strong. She's not going to bolt off and disgrace herself.

I think for a moment of my first time meeting a skrake, of Maeve, standing with me. I shake my head, try to focus.

Nothing comes.

Something *is* coming, though. Big and fast.

It's moments like this you remember how quick it can

all slip away. Moments like this you don't blame people for wanting to die slow behind a wall instead of out in front of it and fast.

This is the worst part, here.

Then it's on us in a blur of teeth, nails and dead fleshy breath, but I know what to do. Aoife bears the brunt of the skrake's attack. It flies at her from nowhere, but she gets her guard up and the skrake only gets its jaws around her forearm, well protected in wraps. Lin is with her already, muscling its head back away from her, slipping her blade . . .

Behind us, another attack, but I've only half-turned when there's one on me too, the weight and the power of it always a surprise. My arms are up and my defence is good. I just have to hold out for Agata, and here she is, nearly levering it off me, and I can wedge up a knee to help her, straining to keep my head clear away from its snapping jaw and evil breath. Agata gets its feet out from under it and by the time we've grounded it we're nearly done, the head nearly gone off it already. It does not take long. I feel very scared. I feel very alive.

Three skrake down to perfect code: teamwork excellent, positioning and focus excellent. It's exhilarating, working like that.

We peer as best we can into the long grass and the shrubs around us but nothing else is moving.

'Check your partners,' Mare says. 'Deep breaths. Stay ready.'

Someone – I think it's Lin – says, 'Airport scum,' and Aoife snorts.

We keep still, though, another while, on alert, waiting.

It's tempting to think the skrake plan an attack all together, when they come from nowhere like that. You can spook yourself wondering if they communicate with each other. They can't use door handles or lay you a trap. Likely those three all ended up out here at the airport and they've been wandering around as a loose pack ever since, attracted by one noise and moving together till they're attracted by another; they mob but only as a matter of accident when nothing has been going on in an area for a while.

This being a theory, anyway, and the one I stick to. I often wonder did anyone ever know for real.

We keep our guards up a long time till Mare at last drops hers and we can follow suit. We relax a little. Sene has found something heavy, a good-sized rock, and she throws it against the glass of one of the rounded clear sides, making Jay jump half out of her skin. It bounces right back at her and anyone looking can see it'll take more than that to smash our way in, but the girl can't resist picking it up and throwing again, hard as she can with all her small strength. It's comical nearly watching her, but we've our game faces on now, we're in high alert, less anything else comes flying out of the long grass at us. Besides which, we'll laugh at anything but a child doing her best.

Aoife goes towards a huge plane of dirty glass to wipe it with her wrapped forearm and peer in. I go to look with her. It's too gloomy to see much; a cavernous space, just a little light coming from high up somewhere.

We form up and move on around the main building, look for a way in. There's nothing. Big squares that look like doors but aren't opening. Growth chokes the building, in some places nearly all the way up to its huge domed roof.

We work till the sun gets low in the sky, circling the whole way round the strange shape of the main building. Mare did good, or Agata did; there'll be useful stuff inside this monster, if only we can crack it open.

In the end we clamber together up the curved sides, using the climbing frame of trees and vines that have grown up high along it. Near the top, on a little platform so high we can see all the surrounding country, we find a break. The roots of some hardy little bush that somehow planted itself up here in a cranny reach down into the void; a bit of metal has come away from a section of the thick glass. We can relax here, with good views around us. Five of us wait, sipping water, while two of us in turns peel the metal lip away from the glass till there's a hole big enough to wriggle through – if you don't mind dropping straight to your death through it. We must be more than two hundred foot above the ground here.

Mare and Sene have pulled rope from their packs, lengths and lengths of it. I haven't seen good rope in years. The rest of us watch, wondering who'll be picked to go down into the darkness.

'I'll do it,' Jay says, her voice high and light and only a little bit shaky in the fading light.

She wants to make up for being new. She wants to impress us. I'm not far behind her on those points and my heart goes out to her.

Lin and Aoife are squabbling quietly about something, Sene peering doubtfully down through the hole. Nobody pays attention so Jay says it again and she keeps saying it till everyone shuts up and listens to her.

'Great,' Lin says. 'Let her risk breaking her back and being eaten alive.' She chews on a fingernail, spits a little out, chews again.

Sene hunkers down beside Jay and speaks to her as if she was a toddler instead of a strapping youth. 'Is that what you want, girlo?'

Jay's skin is so white it's hard to know if she's going paler. She's determined, though, excited, still, by the battle, feeling death-proof. 'I'm the lightest,' the girl says. 'It'll be easier on the rope.'

Sene shakes her head and looks to Mare. We all do.

Mare sighs out through her nose and narrows her eyes at the girl, and as she does I know that she has already thought about it and she is glad the kid volunteered instead of being made to go down. 'You sure about this, Jay? No going back once we get going.'

This, I want to point out, isn't true. There's no reason we can't pull her back in once she's started. Mare is saying this to make sure the kid doesn't start yelling the moment she's let go. I wonder now if this is what Jay was brought along for. Is this why we have a novice with us? I wonder how long Mare would have let things go before asking her outright if she'd do it.

You can back out any time, Jay, I want to say. I fucking don't, though.

Jay smiles back at Mare. 'You'll mind me.'

I swallow and look at Agata, who is very busy pulling her hand wraps tighter.

We get the rope around Jay's little-girl waist. We try to hitch it in such a way that it won't give, while Aoife chatters.

'She'll be on her own once she gets in,' she says. 'If she gets in. Do you think that rope will hold?' Nobody answers but that doesn't stop her. 'I don't like her chances if there are any skrake in there.' A beat. 'Do you think there are skrake in there?'

Nobody answers. We're all more or less used to Aoife's nerves when we're out working. We'll all hold on to the rope, I think. Doesn't matter if there are skrake down there waiting for her – we can lift her out.

'Do a recce, see if you can find a way to let us in. Otherwise, grab what you can and we'll lift you out again,' Sene is advising the girl.

No, I think. No. Suddenly I'm saying it out loud.

'No! Don't.' I'm on my feet and putting my hands out for the rope, drawing Jay back, towards safety. Nobody stops me.

Beside me Aoife says, 'Thank shit,' and I feel a great swell of love for her. Doesn't the world need the loud people as well as the quiet, and don't they have a tougher time of it in this place? Let her speak; let her yell.

I think Mare would have gone on with it anyway, except the kid is already trying to get out of the rope tied around her and Agata is helping her.

'I'll go,' I tell them. 'I'm nearly as light.' It's not true, though I am one of the smallest banshees.

'No,' Agata says, with a vehemence that surprises me. I save taking pleasure in it till later.

'Look, I know you want whatever is in that building. I mean,' I correct myself, 'I know we need it. I'm our best chance.' I'm probably right, which is in my favour, at least. Sene and Mare are stronger, but they're both heavier, and Mare is leader. Aoife and Lin aren't going to volunteer because they're not idiots: they'll save their own skins if ever they can. Their own first, and then each other's, and then maybe ours.

'If there's skrake down there, you think Jay's going to fight them on her own?' What I don't say is that I probably can't either. 'No offence, kid. Look, there's skrake down there, I know there are, and if we lower Jay into them that'll be the end of her and we'll still need whatever it is we need.'

There's a quiet and then Agata, who never says anything at moments like these, says, 'OK.'

'OK,' I say, and I'm a bit disappointed as well because now I'm going to have to do this thing.

Jay will go home this time at least.

There's not a word out of Sene and Mare.

'I'm going too,' Agata says, getting up and putting her hand out for the rope. I want to tell her no, that I want to be able to make decisions that only relate to myself without consideration of her, but I can't find the language and it doesn't seem like the time. Also, I'd like not to go alone.

'There won't be enough rope,' Lin says, biting her nails. Aoife slaps her partner's hand away from her face and then says to the rest of us, 'She's right. Even if there's enough to get you both down all the way, which there isn't, we won't be able to get you back up again, not both at once. Someone will be stuck. You'll be stuck down there, if there's an attack.'

I imagine Lin and Aoife on one rope, tugging me, Sene and Mare on the other, trying to heave our weight upwards while we battle a small army of trapped skrake below. I'm sweating.

'You'll have to halve the rope,' Aoife's saying. 'Is there enough even to get them both safely down?'

Before we know it anyway the rope is being sawn in two with Mare's good serrated knife. I'm panicking too hard now to think things through, but I'm pretty sure that wasn't a good idea. We do our best with our bags. Agata has an old backpack, threadbare and falling to bits with plastic melted over the holes on the inside and one strap hoisted back together with big, clumsy stitches. I've only a squarish fabric bag, rough-sewn by one of the house women, which I wear across my body so my hands are free. It's threadbare, holding little and not holding it well, but I'm only six years old here and I know I'm lucky to have a bag at all. Jay will take years to get good pockets, even.

We check our weapons, and then, without pausing – because if I think too much I'm afraid I'll start begging off, and I cannot do that with Jay's huge eyes on me – I give a nod to Sene and Mare. I set back my weight over the hole in the building's ceiling to make sure they've the slack of the rope in their hands. They set their feet against the solid glass beneath them, gripped against the metal partitions between glass, rope circled around their own bodies.

I do not look down.

I don't want to fucking know.

Suddenly I'm on the finger again in Phoenix City, Boyle's sweet smell hanging over me, a wretched, dying woman's hands brushing mine.

I flex my fingers, breathe out.

I go first through the tight gap and I'm left hanging a moment, every muscle in me straining till I command them to relax, while Agata is organised to come through after me. She lets out a whistling gasp between her teeth as Aoife and Lin ease her down. Agata hates heights. I keep my eyes up, watching the others through the dirty glass as they sweat under our weights.

I wait a little while before I let myself look down. It's much worse than I'd imagined.

In the sludgy green light below, I can make out boxy shapes, platforms with stairs leading to them and away from them. At the bottom of it, far far below, the floor, hard and uncompromising.

It's a long way and if we fall we'll die, though probably not right away. The rope digs welts into my skin as if it's trying to disappear into me in fright. I dig right back. I cling on and try to reassure myself that the rope isn't getting frayed on the edge of the broken pane above me, but the banshees have it resting against a smooth-looking steel bracer and there's nothing I can do about it anyway, I guess.

Nearly half-way, I'd say. I breathe out, swallow, try to relax into the discomfort.

I look over to Agata, who is swinging a little, her eyes screwed shut tightly. Our breaths are loud up here, down here.

Over half-way. We're making good progress.

I whisper, 'We're OK, nearly there.' Agata, nearly level with me, nods, her eyes still shut tight.

Above me, there's a cry, a whirr – and, beside me, Agata falls a few feet in a moment, like someone let go of her ropes. She screams and I look up, squinting against the light, but already she's caught again, stopped. She's grasping the rope tightly, her face bathed in sweat, eyes and mouth wide and horrified. I look up and after a moment we hear it: the laughter, coming from the troop above us.

Even for my love of Agata I cannot help laughing with them.

'Fuckers,' I whisper to show I'm on her side really. Agata looks like she might throw up. Their sniggers follow us the rest of the way down, but even for Agata the tension is gone out of the job, for now. A few feet up off the ground we signal to pause and let our eyes grow accustomed to the gloom. At last we can take a good look around us.

It's a huge glass cage. Light noses in through the broken space above us, and anywhere the foliage hasn't managed to grow on the glass. It's dark and getting darker, and warmer. Things are beginning to grow inside as well as out. Whatever besides us got in through that hole above our heads has done its work, and beneath us wild grass is trying to grow.

It's one long drop from the ceiling where we came in to the ground beneath, but there are other floors as well, built part-way upstairs into the sides. To our left, one of the big platforms leads off somewhere, into another part of the building. Plenty of places for skrake, nevertheless. Better to call out and know now, or to get grounded first and see can we get to them, one by one? I look to Agata and she's already giving the signal to be lowered. A moment after that and we're stopped again. The rope has given out.

It takes time to undo the knots and wriggle out of them with our whole weights working against us, but we're loath to use our knives and split the good rope again. We're both sweating hard by now and it's hot in this big glass dome. But, I'm thinking, if things go wrong, we could maybe build up little stands out of the useless shit in the space around us, reach back up to these ropes, maybe be pulled up one at a time. We won't be in here for ever, one way or the other.

Knots loosened, we drop the last few feet to the ground, using our knees as best we can to lighten the impact. We've no time to enjoy feeling the sodden ground beneath our feet again, though Agata nearly sags with relief. I glance up and I can just make out Mare's face, peering down at us. We move quickly over to the right of the building to put our backs against the glass. We are alone on this little mission now, Agata and me, even if there are five pairs of eyes watching as best they can through the glass. I don't mind it.

'OK?' I ask.

Agata's trying to shrug it off. 'Well, better this than beating up the poor in the shanties,' she says casually, and I stop and just stare at her. I realise it's the first time I've really heard her say something in a long time. She glances at me, gives a little smile, like *of course. Of course* I know what you've been thinking and I've been thinking it too.

The building is so massive it's hard to know how to

clear it. We've agreed silently between us that the best way about this mission is to go quiet, go safe, bring down anything we can in such a way as to not attract the fuckers. There's nowhere to run in here, nowhere to hide. Weapons in hand, we move fast around the perimeter, which takes some time, and then work inwards.

Aoife would say the place is as empty as the space between management's ears. It's a big humid husk, a massive beetle from another age with its legs in the air and its belly rotted out from the inside. There is dust; it smells wild and musty all at once. We're the only ones in here, I'm beginning to think, and after the sun has gone down a finger or two we're moving easier, making more noise, relaxing. On the hunt, always, for a way out, but gathering what we can to make it easier to reach back up to the ropes if we need them. The old world, the before world belonging to the ruiners, is never short of useless junk; we're knee-deep in the shit in some places in the country.

The middle of the glass cavern is taken up with the usual nonsense people of the old world were interested in. Partitions, plastic, none of it making any sense now, if it ever did, functioning only to obstruct. There are clumps that were bodies once and are now just rotted cloth on little hillocks of bad odour. Good enough for them.

We move back again to the right, making a clean sweep through, securing the otherworld of this muggy space as best we can. We find nothing but thick clear doors we can't open leading into the dark, so we secure our weapons and start dragging shelves and partitions to try and make steps back up to the ropes. There's a racket of scraping metal across the floor, but it's a thump from behind us that makes me jump up and out through my skin.

We turn to look and see Aoife's grinning face on the other side of the grimy glass, her fists against the building. She says something to Lin, standing beside her, and they both laugh.

Agata rolls her eyes and we get back to business, back to finding a way out. Building this size, it's not going to be totally closed off. There's always a way through.

We go up steel stairs, testing the solidity of the wall of glass the whole way for weaknesses. There's a bouncing quality to it, even all these years after it was made.

There are metal walls dividing us from the next part of the building and a clump of dusted bodies near them. Trying to get out, they must have been, which bodes well for us.

It's Agata who finds a way through to the next section, though – a whole long series of rubbery tracks behind thick plastic curtains. I wipe at a notice and it says 'Warning. Conveyor.'

Agata, watching me. 'What's it say?'

'You try,' I tell her, wiping off more of the grime so she can see the letters. She sounds out 'Warning' easy enough – she's had practice with that one – but 'Conveyor' stumps her.

'It carries?' I whisper doubtfully in the gloom. 'They were used to carry stuff, probably. I don't see how.'

We crouch down by one of the tunnels, but no matter how much we peer into the darkness we can't see where the tunnel ends. Neither one of us wants to get in a dark contained little space where we can't move or fight. Going who knows where. We stand looking together, and then we look at each other.

I notice suddenly how close to me she is standing, her chest rising and falling, so near that I can inhale the good warm smell of her skin. In the dewy half-light, she is luminous, her lips red, her large, dark eyes resting on me. I watch her as she reaches out a hand and touches my cheek, smooths something away. I inhale sharply.

She steps back, smiling a little, not breaking eye contact.

'Love you,' I say, grinning. It's what we say to each other out here. It stands in for a lot that we haven't spoken about. You don't have the freedom to, back in the city. We're rarely alone together for more than a few moments, and there's so much to say, but then you come out here and it's hard to think of a single thing.

'Love you back, O,' she says, face serious. I like it when she calls me that. She saves it up for me.

If a skrake catches us in here, that'll be it, but there's nothing else for it, no other way out that we can see. We go quiet as we can, but there's the noise of fabric moving fast against our skin, our hands and knees and feet thumping softly on the rubber of the conveyor, the sounds of our breath in the small hot space.

At last I make out a square of blue ahead of us in the black.

'Nearly there,' I say to Agata, moving behind me, my voice just loud enough to be heard.

'I hate this,' she whispers in the dark. 'Heights, small spaces. Not a good day.'

It's so unlike her to admit to any kind of weakness. I don't stop moving but I frown and listen for whatever's coming next.

'Tell me again about the island,' she says at last.

We've talked about my past before, on missions, in barely breathed whispers at night after I first got to the city. She wanted to know everything and eventually I got to trusting her. I told her everything: my mother being turned when I was a girl, and her lover, Maeve, making me kill what was left of her, as training. Then, later, Maeve getting bit. Trying to get her to the city because I'd seen old posters and I realised they were banshees, and maybe they could help us. I wanted to be a banshee too. I didn't want to be alone. Agata is the only one who knows that the runaways the banshees came out of the city chasing got away. She's the only one who saw me help the last of them escape the troop. She's never told anyone.

We have never spoken about that, not once in all these years.

And now I want to, so badly. I stop moving, thinking about the pull that I feel.

'I've been dreaming about them.'

In the heat of the black tunnel I feel the skin on my arms prickle.

I can feel she's listening, but not to me and for a moment I'm so annoyed—

'MOVE!' she screams behind me.

It's not often you'd hear Agata cry out in fear.

I can't see what's coming our way behind Agata, ricketing up behind us along the black tunnel. I can smell it, though.

We're nearly out the other side, a little square of lighter black growing bigger every heartbeat, and I'm thinking this cannot be how it ends. If Agata is bit now I'll just die, I'd want to die.

But I get there and fall out, hands and head first, on to a floor, get my feet under me, reach into the tunnel for Agata and pull.

We both go flying but I put a few hairs of distance between us at least before the skrake is right on top of us. We scrabble off each other to try and get into our guards, seeing which of us it'll go for first. We're dirty, sweating, tired, scared; we're ready more than anything else, however, and we both work slowly away from the tunnel in case anything else comes flying out of it. The skrake, twitching, stinking, follows.

Just enough light to see by, leaking in from who knows where. This one is small, mostly decomposed. There's no skin left, only black and moulding sinew and muscle and scab, as if some poor reaching part of the body it was is still trying to heal. There are a few long strands of hair attached to the scalp and I find these particularly difficult to look at. This was a woman, once. A small woman with long hair, who was doing some business in this place when everything ended. I put that thought aside; it's easier to think of her as a ruiner.

How the creature holds together when it is so rotten is beyond my imagination or reckoning. The proboscis, pink and pulsing and streaked with black, is alive and listening to us, feeling us.

'Why doesn't it—' Agata begins, and it flies at her.

My thoughts are gone. I am only fury and knives. The skrake leaps for Agata and I leap for it, landing on its back, one arm around its neck, pulling backwards, my pins-and-needles legs and feet working to wrap themselves around its legs and sinewy arms. I've my knife out and to its throat and so does Agata, and together we hack and saw at its neck, almost calm now, while the monster lashes and shrieks. We get the skrake down in pretty good time. It was not a strong one.

We gather ourselves quickly and silently, readying our weapons again, prepped to do it all once more if we need to. It's only when we begin to move around I notice Agata is limping. I make her sit down on the ground.

'Shit,' I say, peeling away soaked bandages, trying to get a look at the wound. The monster was behind her, its mouth was right beside her feet, her ankles.

One slip.

'Is it?' I say. 'Agata.'

The tears are coming.

'No,' she says, so quietly I think I imagined it for a moment, but then she takes my hand and she squeezes it and she says, 'Caught it on something jagged.'

I wipe at my eyes with the back of my hand. 'Promise?'

'Yeah,' she says, and she laughs a little and I think it's going to be all right. 'Hurts like a bitch, though, I don't know how much weight I can put on it.'

I help her up and she tries it out, winces.

'We need to leave,' she says, and in the near-dark, we look at each other, faces close together.

Closer.

Her breath on my mouth, my nose.

'Don't we?' she says.

I move my head closer to hers, just a fraction, and she lowers hers and our foreheads touch and we just stay that way, quiet for a while.

She's waiting for me to say something. I'm confused; I don't know what I want.

'Agata,' I whisper.

She smiles at me. 'O,' she says. Nothing more.

We can't find where the light is coming from and after a while we get bored of trying to feel our way around. There's nothing for it but to get into the tunnel again and crawl back to the cavernous glasshouse we landed in first. A skrake got in there somewhere so one could come back out again and we go one at a time now through the tunnel, me first because I'm not injured.

It takes a long time for Agata to come through once I give the all-clear. She's hurt badly. I don't call out till she's back by my side but when I see the state of her in the light, pale and sweaty and beat, I feel like I should have. I want to get her back behind walls.

In the end we don't even have to shout. They come for

us anyway. Hungry fuckers. I smell them first, then see them, the far side of the ropes, coming through the vents, scratching and tearing themselves through metal to get to us.

I pull Agata back to where the two ropes dangle off the ground. Not safety, but a little light, and familiarity at least. I look up and they're still there. I'm grateful for that, even if they can't help us.

'Incoming!' I shout up at them, 'Incoming!' And then I turn to face them.

One skrake, close, two others coming. There may be more; the tunnels slow them a little bit at least. We'll be all right if Agata isn't too injured to fight. We might still be all right.

We've time to look at each other and I see right away that it isn't going to be all right. She's in pain, and she's frightened.

First skrake coming at us now, and Agata and I form up as best we can.

In the corner of my eye I see one of the ropes twitch and then move and I glance up, blinking against the light.

The banshees are coming.

Before I can take it in – their reaching for the ropes with no safety or support or practice or training for this particular situation – there's a skrake on Agata and I get to work.

We're rounding on our second when I become aware of the height and power of Mare and Sene landing and taking on the third, and the uncanny teamwork of Aoife and Lin backing us up.

There are four skrake in the end and once we get into a rhythm we dispatch them till the flat hard ground beneath our feet is slippery with blood and black gore, the two other teams a little out front, protecting us.

We stand firm, guards raised, waiting to see will more come.

'Where's Jay?' Aoife wants to know, and Mare raises her eyes to the ceiling. The tiny face peers down at us. I'm glad she didn't try to make it down, she'd have done no good, and it's better to have someone on the outside. She surely couldn't make it back up again on those slim little arms of hers besides. Even with all our own practised strength, climbing that far up on rope is going to take everything we have left.

We wait, holding tight to our guards, till Mare is satisfied there's nothing else coming for now and she drops her fists.

'Any news?' Aoife asks, and Lin laughs a little shakily.

I take Agata by the arm away from the worst of the gore and help her down gently.

'We've an injury here,' Agata says clearly so everyone will hear. So that I don't have to. 'Skin is broken.'

Sene reaches for her knife and I hate her for that but I pretend I do not see and I hope that Agata doesn't notice.

There's nothing Agata does not notice.

It's code anyway, it's form. It's how things are done.

I might hate Sene sometimes, and Mare too, but I don't envy her her work.

I ease off the sticky cloth from Agata's shin once more and she breathes tightly through her teeth. I keep lifting away till everyone can see exactly what's happened.

No way this could be construed as a bite. It's a tear of skin, deep, bleeding a lot still.

But procedure is that Sene checks it herself, and then Mare checks it, and I don't let myself breathe a full lungful while they do it.

'You sure it's not a bite?' Mare says, looking real close.

'Hey, fuck you,' says Lin, and Sene gives her a shove, a hard one.

'Got caught in the tunnels is all,' Agata says, her voice strained but calm.

'It's true,' I say, but I feel that it doesn't matter too much what I say just then. They know I'd lie for Agata.

Agata lies back, letting Mare poke around the wound a little more.

'Agata,' she says.

'You know I'd say if I got bit. I wouldn't bring that shit back with me and you *know* that.'

'We all know that,' Aoife says, her voice kind. She's right as well.

'You come out in a fever, we'll have to put you down,' Mare says.

'We better make sure it doesn't swell up then,' I say, and reach for my shitty little bag so I can try to clean the wound and patch it up with what I've got.

Mare sighs, considering, and then moves away to let me at it. I work away quietly, trying not to think about how close we came to everything ending. How close we are still. It's easy to forget that sometimes. Everything can change in an instant. Everything might have changed already, if Agata doesn't heal up well, if she can't keep working.

'Lin just told me she wants your shoes when you die,' Aoife says, and we laugh, Agata too. We start feeling like a team again and already the others are checking their way around for a way out.

'Could be stuck here,' Lin is saying soft to Aoife, and I look up again at the height they all came down, just on ropes, to help us. I could cry.

'We should build up to the ropes,' I say. Agata and I did our best to stack the shit we could find beneath them so we could make a jump for them if we needed to, but it all came crashing apart when the banshees landed.

I see Mare and Sene exchange a look and I blush, thinking I've overstepped, but then in a raised eyebrow I understand something else instead.

We start gathering up again what we can find to make getting up to the bottom of the ropes easier if we are in a hurry. By the time we're finished we're all sweating and thirsty, and still none of us is happy about the exit. Agata's not going to be able to climb, probably, is what we're thinking. We need to find another way out.

In the end there's nothing for it but the tunnel again.

Jay won't be left alone: she yells down at us that she's coming, and when she doesn't hear Sene tell her to stay where she is, or Lin swearing at her, she does hear Mare directing her to throw down the supply bags.

There's a pause.

'You hear me, Jay?'

'I'll throw them down if I can come down.'

Sene swears under her breath while Aoife starts laughing. I catch Lin's look, eyebrow raised. We're all impressed.

The bags are dropped and the kid is told to haul up one rope and tie it around her for safety, then to grab on to the other and start lowering herself down, hand over fist. I wonder are we doing the right thing, letting her come to us. I'd be frightened too, staying out all night on that little platform on my own in the cold, but even still. Could we stop her?

She does so well till the rope runs out and then doesn't leave enough bounce in her legs for a good landing; she turns her ankle, falls, a puff of air going out of her that we can all hear. She gives herself a moment to right herself and when she does she has tears in her eyes and her hands are shaking but she still smiles at us and she says, 'I knew I could do it.'

No injuries in weeks and then two bad legs in one shitty afternoon.

No one says anything back to her and I feel bad so I find myself reach out a hand, ruffling her hair. 'You did good, kid.'

Eventually, we find riches.

All around us, under the dust, a cornucopia of bright colours, packaging, bottles and boxes. I blink and look at Agata, who is staring at me, grinning. It's untouched, all of it.

Mare is glassy-eyed.

'All right, pack up! Stay within crying distance. We haven't secured the space.'

Lin gives a shout when she finds a whole wall of backpacks. Dusty but intact, padding on the shoulders, different compartments inside for your stuff. We could walk for days with bags like these. We load up, trying to carry enough for several troops.

It's in a dark corner with the light almost gone that I find what I've been looking for these last six years. Toothbrushes, still in their packaging, a dozen of them. Smaller than I remember, or differently made, but they'll do. I stuff them in my backpack along with squidgy bars of soap, a couple of dusty books. All around me there's the happy noise of looting, the rustling sounds of the goods of another age being rifled through and desecrated and made our own.

There's a clank of glass and Agata calls me to her. She's found a low shelf of clear bottles with something sloshing in them still. I hunker down beside her. Carefully, glancing around, she opens one, smells. I expect her to wince. She puts her lips to the bottle, lifts it a little, passes it to me. The bottle feels cool to the touch though everything in this tomb must have been the same temperature for decades now. I take the smallest sips of the liquid so clear it could be good water. It burns; my lips, my tongue, my throat, but then the heat it gives is nearly pleasant.

A slips a hand into her backpack, brings out some cloth, wraps the bottle in it and slips it back in, winking at me.

'Got you.' Mare towers over us with a leer. 'Found the

good stuff, hah?' She raises her voice so we can all hear. 'A bottle or two for management is fine but don't cram up your packs with it. We've better things to be taking home with us.'

Once she's gone again Agata takes a glug, coughs and laughs beside me.

'Better than the poitín those farmers make,' she says. I love it when she does this, disobeys. It's so rare and so pure. When Aoife hears us, too far across the room to know even why we're laughing, she joins in.

We make the area as secure as we can; we designate an area for pissing and shitting. We'll billet comfortably on the clothes we find around us – more comfortable than a banshee has any right to expect on an overnight mission. More comfortable than we'd be back at barracks. There's no fire, no light to see by, but it's still warm. Only Mare and Sene are holding us off from bringing out a clear bottle of something to share amongst us. We're all down to our small-clothes in the heat.

'We could live out here,' Jay says out of nowhere, and we all round on her.

'Have you no learning, girl?' says Aoife, her voice appalled.

'Watch that mouth or you'll be for a punishing,' Mare tells her.

Poor Jay, frightened, mortified, says quickly, 'I mean, for the city. With the city, like . . . a little city. With management and everything.'

'Pff, with no walls?' Sene. 'The city's the only safe place, the only place that can last. It's the pain in your foot, girl, making you wild.'

Usually there's a long silence if anyone talks about starting up outside the city, after everyone has said how impossible it is. Rare enough it's brought up. I'm beginning to think: is that silence that comes to do with me? People remember who I am then and where I came from. I stay quiet back is all I can do. I glance at Agata but I can't see her expression in the dark.

I dream my dream of home. I'm getting closer to it, closer to my mothers every time. A warm hearth, the smell of coddle, potatoes and seaweed, and something else too. Warm dog. I can see Maeve and Mam, in the distance, sitting with their heads together on the beach – but the waves are coming and I can't . . .

I'm awake. It takes me a few moments to calm, to remember where I am. It is just getting light and I can hear low voices murmuring. For a little while I don't stir; I let the dream recede a little and try to think instead of the coming brightness, the warmth, the feeling of my troop and only my troop around me. The feeling we can get up and make the day ours.

Thirsty. The heat of the place, and the clear stuff didn't help. Need to piss.

Agata is not beside me; I knew it as soon as I woke, but now it's light enough to see her bedding. I reach out a hand and feel how cold it is and I listen harder to the murmuring to distinguish her voice. Rub the sleep out of my eyes, and go quietly looking. Sene is in a ball, sleeping. Aoife too, a tuft of her spikey reddish hair sticking up towards the ceiling.

'Hall' is the word I want to use for where we are. Too large to be a room, but with bits sectioned off, the mini-shops and seating areas, with other halls leading off it for huge bathrooms. A corridor, nearly. Not like anything I've seen before in scale and design. A way to get from one place to another, hardly a place in itself. Big windows everywhere, almost too grimy to be letting in light, but there isn't much dust. Not too much dust means not too many corpses, and that usually means not too many skrake. It's a good place.

I'm up, trying to remember which space we designated for latrines, yawning and rubbing my head. Feeling bad for feeling free.

At a turn I see Jay, standing awkwardly at a corner, hiding her body behind the wall while she peeks around it. I go silently up behind her and see what she's hiding from – listening to. A quiet talk between Mare, Lin and Agata.

I feel pinched Agata is there without me.

I creep up behind Jay, staying out of sight of the group so I don't alarm them, and watch Jay as she watches, her lithe little form still as glass. Pretend that I'm not creeping with her.

Agata is speaking low and fast.

'She can fix the water issue. She can, trust me on that. She's not the issue. If we were to leave—'

I start. This is not a conversation that should be overheard, and I touch Jay's shoulder. She jumps about two inches in the air, and gasps with pain when she turns on her bad ankle.

'Morning,' I say blandly, loudly, when she has nothing but a guilty face for me. 'Sleep well?'

She nods and breathes out and starts moving back towards our little camp. I raise my eyebrows, watching her go, and when I glance towards the group I see they're watching her too. Mare's face is like thunder, but then, that's her face.

I watch Jay till she's out of sight and then go to sit amongst them, Agata shifting over to let me on a cushioned bench beside her, she nursing her wounded leg.

'How long was she hiding there?' Mare asks, and I shrug.

'Long enough, I'd say. I only just woke up. What did I miss?'

There's silence for a moment and Agata says gallantly, 'Water. We were just saying we've found none.'

I nod. Why does she keep lying to me? 'We'll have to find our way out of here today so.'

Mare nods. 'We'll gather up the last supplies, and we'll keep looking. There'll be a way.'

There's a silence. I make it awkward, I know I do.

'How much trouble are we in here?' I risk asking. Trapped with little to no water in what is basically a big greenhouse. Even if Jay had stayed outside of it and gone back for help, what could anyone do? Another troop might lift us out if there was enough rope left in the city. But Jay did not stay outside, so there's nobody to tell where we are.

'We'd no permission for the mission,' Mare says calmly.

I stare, open-mouthed, feeling as if the earth has come up and smacked me. I can't take it in, the truth of what she's telling me.

'If we bring back the goods, we'll get a welcome,' Sene says.

I look at her and she catches me, smiles. Stoic as ever.

* * *

124

We work on our search, each of us carrying sturdy packs now, bursting with clothes, hats, socks, glass bottles, shoes, utensils, whatever valuable thing we can each put our hands on. Enough to maybe keep Mare from being punished if we get back to the city. Agata spends most of her time picking up lengths of plastic piping and carries them around with her. We're all geared up in completely fresh outfits, Jay so excited about her first loot that she's glassy eyed. I don't want to tell her that she probably won't be let keep any of it. Plenty more experienced banshees will need it ahead of her. I try and look out for something I can swipe and hide for her, something I can give her to keep once we're back.

The smell of skrake comes and goes, but for a long time we see nothing and hear nothing.

We switch out the best of our supplies as we go if we find better, but we're keen again to find a way out, safe and all as it feels here. We get thirsty is one thing – in the warmth of the glass building we all feel cooked after a few hours of daylight.

We find: endless packages of food, nearly all useless, but some yielding a golden yellow liquid, delicious and almost unbearably sweet. So many bags we despair of going through them all, and Mare tells us to leave them for the next troops.

We find endless side-rooms, windowless and airless

and smelling like death. Lin makes a map as she goes, in her head but reliable for that, and she leads us left and left again, and gets us to help her bash in a door and then another. We find ourselves back in the first huge hall, the rope hanging from our entrance place.

'Might be our only way out,' Aoife says, her voice worried. We all think of Jay and Agata's injuries. Agata's arm strength is lethal – she might make it without use of her feet to help her climb – but Jay hasn't a chance. Getting Jay back up there will need teamwork.

We keep looking.

We begin to wonder is there any way out at all, or will we be stuck here. With no water we'll be dead in three days – sooner even, this place so warm. The food we've found, crackers in packets, sweet biscuits, doesn't help with the thirst, it only makes it worse. We hold off eating more. It is a hot slog and we are hungry and thirsty.

Eventually we open the wrong door.

The skrake have kept quiet in one of those windowless rooms, a whole horde of them.

The room is a mess, and by the glimpse I get when we open the door I can see the whole sorry story of what happened. A group in there, and one by one they were all got, and then they all turned. The few weeks of the agony of turning, all of them together; the shitting and the dying. No way out, locked in tight. Trying to take care of each other while they went. Or not.

We broke the door so thoroughly off its hinges to get into the room that we cannot close it again when we see what is inside. There's nothing for it but to run, and there's nowhere to run but back to the ropes.

There are too many of them, and we are slow, laden down with our packs. Stuff we'd risk our lives to keep.

I have time to register Sene streaking ahead.

Agata is moving, I can see. She's OK; she's practised at working through injuries. It might fuck her recovery, but she's a survivor.

Jay is slow. Too slow. She'll be got, I realise in a bleak moment of understanding. There's nothing any of us can do about that.

Mare brings up the rear and she keeps turning to throw whatever she can in the way of the skrake, but in these vast corridors there are no doors.

We were careless is what happened, and you cannot be careless in this world. I was raised knowing this, but too long in the city, not enough missions, I got careless.

We make it, somehow, through the little room that leads back to the big hall, Mare pulling us through desperately while she gets ready to try and close the door against them. I stay with her, letting the two injured go on with Aoife and Lin. The door will not hold, it swings both ways, but we buy enough time to get them almost to the ropes, Aoife and Lin nearly carrying the girl between them.

'Find something,' I yell, 'Find something to push back against the door!'

But there is nothing: anything we could have found quickly we need to get us up high enough to reach the ropes. We hold as best we can, every second helping the others get away.

Sene is nearly half-way up the rope already, I can see her outlined against the green and muck of the glass, her muscled arms pumping smoothly, moving so fast it seems like a dream.

Aoife and Lin reach the bottom of the ropes; Aoife climbs up the rickety structure we've made, pulling Jay after her and even putting her little hands to the rope on the left, and there's something about the movement that breaks my heart. Aoife gets started on the right rope, pulling herself up with great grunts. It's the best thing she can do for the team, for the city, even, at this point, if you believe in that kind of thing.

Watching Aoife go up, Jay manages to pull herself metres into the air in just a few moments. Then she fumbles, falls, yells when she lands on her ankle. Lin is with her now, putting the rope in her hands again, shouts something at her I can't make out. Getting a shoulder under her to try and boost her up. It's better than I expected from Lin, to be honest, and I don't mean that in a bad way.

Agata is still working her way up the rickety pile of crap to the ropes.

Beside me Mare shouts at Lin to go up after Aoife, and after a moment, after seeing Jay back on her rope and a few feet in the air at least, Lin obeys.

There's nothing for it but for Mare and myself to tear it to the ropes.

Sene has made it to the roof and she's trying hard to pull the rope up after her; I see now what she was thinking, running ahead: that she could help the weakest of us up behind her. She can do nothing with the one rope with Lin and Aoife on it, but she could raise up the one with Jay grasping on . . .

If only Jay could hold on long enough, but just ten feet up her strength is failing, and before Sene can start to tug her up, she lets go, falls hard, screams.

I need Agata to get on to a rope. She's tooling around with that fucking length of pipe she found, trying to strap it on her back.

'Go!' shouts Mare, and I see her brace herself against the door.

'No!' I yell back. I know she can't hold it on her own.

'Go!' she shouts again, and I obey, knowing she'll have a plan, knowing she's right behind me.

I sprint towards the ropes, feeling the skrake breaking through behind me but I've only eyes for Agata. She's on a rope, the pipe strapped to her backpack.

I start to climb, trying to work hard enough so that when Mare comes behind me she can get high enough quickly, out of the way of the skrake's grasps.

We're out of time. For long moments that are just short breaths I'm all pull and sweat, heaving myself arm over arm, my feet working to find each other and put the rope between them and push upwards, getting purchase as best I can.

It is a long way, it is harder work even than I thought it'd be, the hardest physical thing I've done in years. Ever, maybe. I thought I was sweating already but it's pumping out of me now, getting into my eyes, dripping between my breasts and down my back.

I make slow progress but I'm safe, safe enough up here.

The rope bucks under me and I clutch it harder, panicked for a moment that I'll fall, and then I see that beneath me Mare is climbing and I heave a breath and work on upwards. I give myself five more heaves before I let myself look to the other rope.

Jay is still on the ground. I'm glad Mare did the thing she had to do and saved her own life if she could not save the child's. She'd have put the rope in the kid's hands again and then got on it herself. If the skrake weren't directly behind her she'd have made a loop for her one good leg, maybe. Maybe if there was just a little more time we could have pulled her far enough up, we could have figured it out.

Jay's screams do not go on for long. We all look away as the skrake tear into her. We look upwards. We climb, and I wonder, am I the only one thinking that it is good she gave us a few moments to get higher up, to get away from them.

All silent, we keep going, and above me Aoife and Lin have met Sene on the roof and all three of them are pulling up Agata's rope. She overtakes us and I stop a moment to catch a breath, to watch her reach the jagged glass lip of the hole and be worked carefully through. She is safe.

In another few moments the four of them have our rope, and Mare and I hold tight and let ourselves be pulled up out of that place, heavy bags and all.

We sit together afterwards, huddled in our gloom on the little platform we started out from, waiting to be ready to start our trek back to the city. Miserable as we are, finished as we feel, we all know we cannot wait long. We are too thirsty.

Aoife is crying, the first thing in her life she's done quietly, maybe, and Lin puts an arm around her, draws her close.

Nobody has anything to say.

We re-shoulder our packs. Good gear. Nothing worth a life, though it might save Mare's. A greenun lost . . . For these goods, for a new territory other banshees can come and finish ransacking, she'll get away with it. We work our way back out of the airport and turn south, our tongues thick in our mouths.

What's the life of a little girl, after all?

Though we're coming at the city from the north, we've to swing our way around on a long stretch of raised path the banshees call the Ring Road so we can approach it the usual way, from the south.

I keep an eye on Agata, wanting to be sure she's keeping up OK, and half expecting her to make some excuse to get us away from the others. She keeps her head down as if we're going back to the city after any other mission. Carrying that pipe with her still.

I am familiar with this place on the Ring Road. We're a few clicks out of the city, near the land mines. For me this place is haunted. I have taken a little habit of resting here, of saying hello to my ghosts. Even today, thirsty though we are, they let me stop to leave a stone beside the bush where I murdered Maeve, my second mother.

I'm allowed a few moments of quiet, a time with no push and pull, though by now the sun is sinking and we all have white scum around the corners of our mouths. We are all tired. I put one more stone on top of the other, a good pile now, and count how many times I've been out on mission since I killed Maeve, or let her be killed, trying to get to the city. The stones tell me how many times I've been free in these last six years. A sturdy little pile telling the story of my survival while people around me disappear.

How many more times will I come back here to lay another stone on top of the others? How long till we lose another? Till we lose one another? Mare and Sene, Aoife and Lin. Agata. Cold and powerful, warm and loving, imperfect: our own.

Agata knows this big sad pile of stones is all I have instead of a loved one, bones that should be buried deep in the earth beside the remains of the mother I came out of, her lover. The *shinaun* on that desolate and beautiful island in the west we came from crying out for her. I could have interlaced their skeletal fingers, their feet. They would have lived happier if they could have died knowing I'd do that.

They'd have lived happiest if they could know I was safe.

I've failed them in nearly every way I could. I let myself cry and it starts out being for Jay but it ends up being just for me. The others stand awkwardly back, pretending not to see, but Agata kneels down beside me and I rest my face on her shoulder.

When I'm finished, I wipe my eyes and sniff and smile, self-conscious, but Agata is staring at me full force back, her dark eyes huge in the warm light, her lips red and her brown skin nearly glowing. I never saw a woman who wasn't sometimes beautiful, but Agata always is. The thought of going back to the city now with no idea of when we'll be let out again, or how much Mare might be punished or lauded for leading this mission, is a black haze hanging over us.

Lin kneels beside us and, low and quiet, begins a stream of words I cannot understand. Aoife kneels with her, her eyes closed. I withdraw a little. The shrine is no longer just mine. It's theirs and it's Jay's too. Agata holds out her hand to me and together we get up from the shrine to leave Lin and Aoife.

'Her mother died early as well,' Agata whispers to my good ear. 'Lin's. Herself and Aoife, they try and remember the language they were taught by her.'

I watch them, huddled together around a shrine that isn't theirs – or isn't just mine any more.

'Some mothers let go of their children,' Agata goes on

quietly. 'Mine did: she'd ten children in a dozen years; she couldn't keep up with us. I was lucky I was taken on by Ash when I was. But others, they'll hold on, if they can. They were closer to her when the flux got her and their other sisters. Father was involved, from what I hear.'

These new confidences, instead of making me feel closer they're showing me how far apart we are. There's so much she's been holding back from me. I love her still. Something happened between us in that tunnel, something new was made. Just as I open my mouth to whisper back to her, she says, as if she was saying that she thought it was going to rain, loud enough for the others to hear, 'When are we going to talk about leaving?'

I expect the reaction to be shocked.

It is not. I watch Mare, especially. She rubs her hands back and over the short spikes of her hair, she rubs her face, she sits down, and Sene follows and then Aoife and Lin do the same.

A little circle around the shrine.

'We'll talk about it now,' Mare says.

'At last.' Aoife's the first to speak, which shouldn't surprise. 'What were you at?' She's looking at me.

'Waited long enough,' Lin says, sounding genuinely annoyed.

'Do we go now?' Mare asks Agata.

135

'No,' Agata says, impatient. 'I told you, there's things we need in the city.' I never heard anyone be impatient with Mare before and it's like I've opened a door to another world.

Six years. Six years and I always believed it was Mare and Sene in charge.

'What more do we need?' Lin says, gesturing at our stuffed backs. 'Don't want to go back in that city. We could catch that new plague, all of us.' There's the noise of her biting her fingernails again and Aoife reaches forward, pulling her hand away from her mouth. 'Stop!'

'You stop,' Lin says.

'You asked me to stop you.'

'I thought it was just you and me.' I can hardly look at Agata. The words come out of me without warning and my voice sounds weird and tight. True words, though.

There's silence.

'Not much of a life, just the two of us,' Agata says, after a moment. She smiles a little, reaches for my hand.

I move away. 'How long have you all been talking about this?'

'Maybe four years now?' Sene says after a moment.

'I think everyone started thinking about it when we found you,' Agata goes on. 'It took a while for us all to come to the same conclusion. Then longer for us to say it to each other.'

'We'd to wait for you,' Lin says, rolling her eyes.

'Why?' My eyes are filling with tears. I will not, I will *not* look at Agata, though I know that over to my right she's staring at me.

'We need you,' she tells me, in nearly a whisper.

'We wanted you to speak first,' Mare says, her voice clipped. 'If we told you what we were thinking you could have gone to management. You know what happens to people who want out, who say they want out.'

'Specially now,' Lin says. 'With management taking an interest in you.'

'I told them,' says Agata. 'I trust you, and we're running out of time.'

You didn't trust me enough, I want to say, but I leave it. There's too much else going on.

'Because of the plague,' Lin says.

'And Boyle,' Mare says. 'Murdering two banshees right off.'

'He frightens me,' Sene puts in.

'You need me?' I say. I know already it's not because I'm good with a knife.

'You've lived out here,' Mare says. That's what it always comes down to, it's what people are always curious about. 'Agata says you know a place, an island.'

My eyes fly to hers now. Of course. I told her all my secrets.

They were secrets.

She opens her mouth to say something but I won't let her. 'Then you know there's a problem with water. There was hardly enough for three of us, and that was years ago.'

This, of course, being what the three of them were talking about back at the crack of dawn. Back when Jay was still alive.

'Is that why you let her die?' I ask Mare.

When Mare gets up I don't flinch, and I should have. She takes two steps forward, leans down a little, and punches me clean in the face. Slaps, really – it's open handed – but it's such a blow my jaw cracks and I stop crying.

'Stop,' Agata says, like we don't have time for this.

I won't tell them that there might be three people or even four living out there now. I won't ask Agata if she told everyone that as well.

'I might have an answer to that,' Agata says.

'We can't go now,' I say, nearly to myself, thinking it through again. The temptation to turn and go is so strong. Even with Mare.

'Can't muster enough piss to get working in my canteen,' Lin says, and that's true for all of us.

'We know there's no water too near here, and anyway, my answer to the water question is back inside the city,' Agata says.

'Who goes?' I ask. 'Us and who else?'

There's silence, even from Agata now. She wants to bring more people. I'm not enough. Fine.

I know that she's not enough for me either. I know that one person can't be everything to another, but I'm tired and have a headache and a heartache, and I let myself feel it for a little while. She's been telling my secrets, and that changes things.

Then I swallow and look at the stones again, and I think of Maeve and Mam, getting out on their own so long ago. Just the two of them, striking off across the country, relying only on each other. I think of the lonesome life we had; I think of that terrible pull, that terrible hunger I had in me to find others.

Agata is right, no matter how I feel about it.

'We can't do it alone,' I say quietly.

'Do what?'

'Survive,' I say.

'We can. We survive out here alone all the time,' Aoife says. 'Imagine if we found somewhere defensible, somewhere we could sow crops, with water, with no skrake—'

'There's nowhere like that,' Lin says.

'There is,' I say. 'There is if we've enough water. But what then? We live for a while and then die, and that's it?'

'That's life,' Sene says darkly.

'Good enough for me,' Aoife says.

'What about the future, what about what comes after us?'

Lin just snorts and gesticulates at the wilderness around us. Like, nothing's coming after this.

I take a deep breath. Enough silences.

'I was brought up by two runaways,' I tell them, and the quiet changes a little. I never talk about where I came from but they know it all anyway. Maybe they'll feel differently if they hear it from me. 'One of them was pregnant with me. They found an island off the west coast. I've no idea if they knew about it or just lucked upon it. They didn't tell me anything. But they kept me safe and they tried to make me happy. They were banshees and that's why I am . . . the way I am. That's why when I saw a banshee poster—'

'"Making the World Safe for You",' says Aoife, making her voice deep and loud.

'Tss,' goes Lin, in disgust.

I put my hands in front of me on the dry earth, trying to find the words. Can't stay out here right now. Can't stay in the city, even if we wanted to. Things are crumbling, coming to an end. I feel caught on all sides, and I've been here before, a place with no good options and hardly a choice except put one leg in front of the other. This is what I felt, running to Phoenix City six years ago.

But we've got to do better. We've got to try and save more than ourselves.

The others are watching me carefully and I rub my hands through my short hair and open my mouth to—

'Oh, this is going to be a whole thing—' Lin interrupts. Aoife belts her one.

'I felt like I recognised myself and found something to try and live up to. I knew what we had: we were safe, but it wasn't enough. And those posters I saw, they must have gone up all over Ireland way back when. It worked on me, I guess. When they died, Mam and Maeve, I was on my own and I had no choice – I couldn't stay there by myself.'

That's not the whole truth. Mam got bit and Maeve made me use her as practice killing. Then I made Maeve show me the mainland, and she got bit, but even then I wouldn't let her go to die back on the island and rest with my mother. I made her come towards Phoenix City. The truth is always more complicated.

'She's right,' Agata says. 'We have to bring more people.' She's being short. She's waiting for us to finish the argument and all land on her correct opinion.

'People like who? Banshees are the only ones who ever want to get out,' Sene says. 'I never talked to anyone else who wanted to get out.'

'We're never let talk to anyone,' Agata points out. 'Took Orpen this long to say it to us even.'

'And it's not true,' I say, thinking while I do, that it was actually Agata who spoke. 'I know there are others. I know – I know that we should at least ask. They'll die in there.'

'They'll die out here,' Mare says.

'Their choice,' Lin shrugs.

She wants the fastest way out. Aoife too, probably. Take everyone, leave everyone – she doesn't care.

'Those stupid posters,' I say quietly. 'We could make them real.' I look up to each of the banshees around me. 'We could try . . . to protect, to save.'

'When we go back missing a greenun, we might never get out on a mission again,' Sene says. 'Mare will be demoted, and probably me too, and that's if we're not punished.'

'Not with this stuff,' Lin says, determined, gesturing at our stuffed bags.

I look to Agata – we all do – and she's nodding.

I agree with her: I think they'll be OK, but it's a risk. New leaders are unpredictable.

'And what do you think they'd be like out here, breeders, farmers?' Mare says. 'No training, no experience. They'll be dead weight. We can't carry the dead.'

Agata is looking at her hands. 'We need them, though.

They need us but we need them too – people who know how to farm and build.'

Lin takes a deep breath in, lets it out. 'OK, so we're going to live on an island off the coast, the island you're from, Orpen.'

I nod. 'It's safe enough. There'll be a problem with water – there won't be enough for all of us – and I don't know much about crops and things . . .'

'But first,' Aoife holds up a finger, 'We need to tell anyone who wants to come to pack up and head on out with us. And then we just, what? Escape?'

'We don't need an escape,' I tell the troop. And again I find I'm speaking without realising where I'm going to land, like the rest of me got there well before my head did, or like it's Mam or Maeve speaking *through* me. Calling me home again. 'We need a revolt.'

The Way Back

THERE IS A STORY OF A WITCH WHO LIVES IN THE VERY north, a powerful woman who has learned to use the skrake for her own ends.

This woman lives in the woods, in a cabin by a stream, tending her fowl and her garden. She keeps company with her dogs, the forest animals, birds and deer, and the skrake, which do not harm her, but help her catch little children.

It's a story the breeders tell their children, I understand, though why children need any stories more frightening than the skrake to keep them quiet in the city I don't know. Frightening women are maybe easier to imagine if you've never seen a skrake.

The story changes, I suppose, when the girls grow into women and have their own. They retell the story from what they can remember or imagine. It's the only way to pass down these stories, the only way in which they can be kept, for women who are not taught to read.

Just one generation without learning and it's gone for ever. Whoever made the decision not to teach the next girls to read – some time after my mothers, Mam and Maeve, escaped from the city – they knew what they were doing. Whatever knowledge can be got from the older generations, whatever might have been learned from the books, is gone. For the women, at least, and the men, too, in the shanties and on the wall. For us, nothing new can be learned. Nothing old can be kept pristine. Old words and ideas are turned over and passed along by story, by voice, in a city where women are voiceless. But there's beauty there too, in stories carried only by memory, from past to present to future. There's a type of learning there as well, in what each voice brings to the stories.

These are the thoughts I have as we make our laborious way back in.

Behind me, Mare stumbles, her hands tied and a blindfold on. She knows where she's going better than any of us but we are doing things by the book. You never know what might have changed in the city since we were gone – a newer leader even than Boyle, a fire, a skrake – and we don't know for sure we won't meet anyone else out here, unlikely though it seems.

So, Sene and Mare say their goodbyes, foreheads resting against each other for a moment, and I take the lead as troop leader. I wanted Agata but she said me. The others went with her. It'll be Ash or management, I suppose, who make the final call, or at least it would be if we were staying.

This is the plan we have made. Sene will report Mare for speaking about her wish to leave. We'll back her up. Mare will be punished. When the city is gathered by Boyle in a day or two or whenever he decrees, he'll ask me to speak again. I'll ask everyone if they want to go, and I say that we'll protect people wanting to leave, as best we can. Like we're supposed to. And then – we'll just go.

We're relying on being right about the people being at breaking point, that the wallers and the farmers will be with us. We're relying on some of the banshees at least joining us. We're relying on a lot.

The plan feels already stunningly naïve, but after I suggested it and before people could say stop or change their minds, we were bundling up Mare and here we are.

We file out, one after the other, make our final approach back in, heading down into the long, wet dark of the tunnel. Even if we didn't have to be silent, we've nothing to say to each other now.

I'm not sure any of us thinks it'll work.

But this plan, these terrible few days we have ahead of us now, is the one chance we have, the only one we seem to be able to make for ourselves.

We cannot leave. We cannot go back to barracks and wait to be told to go and break up homes and faces in the shanties. We cannot come out here again with a greenun hanging out of us.

It's often the way, I've found, with choices: it's not a decision to do something, it's a need not to have to do something else.

I think again about the witch of the north, living her quiet life, unmolested, alone with her thoughts. I wonder where that story started; were Mam and Maeve told it when they were children? Did they leave to find her, or become like her?

There were deer here in Phoenix City once, someone told me, probably Agata. It's so hard to imagine anything good and pure and wholesome in this place. And then the thing that happens to good things here: they were ate. I remember, six years ago now, the huge deer with the antlers I saw on the road, being chased by skrake. I wonder was it ever caught, by people or by the skrake. It probably doesn't make much difference to the deer.

We're ravenous like them, I think. We're manipulative like them. They didn't lick that off the stones.

I think with longing of that woman in the woods. Maybe if we somehow get out alive I'll manage it, a space to myself, a clean, good-smelling refuge where I can be alone and think quietly of the people I've lost one way or another along this road. I can dream of people without having to be with any. Nobody will have to watch my loneliness. Five years ago, three even, I maybe wouldn't trust myself to live a life alone and now it's the only way I can imagine myself being happy.

There's a feeling you get when you're back in the city after a mission, when you've been through it and come out the other side while others, your friends, have not. It's relief but it's fright as well. There's a fear that this'll be your last time coming in safe, that next time your friends will be mourning your loss.

Still, I feel more at home heading towards the great beyond than coming back in here.

It's hard not to think about *home* home, not just how the island might be now, but back to how it was when I was a child and I had my mothers loving me. Every moment that passes gets me further away from it and there's nothing at all I can do about it.

This feeling is always at its worst in this moment,

standing on the platform back into Phoenix City, still stinking of the tunnel, so thirsty. I couldn't go around letting myself acknowledge this feeling every day, and I don't. I need to sleep for about a week to take in everything that's happened, but Mare's bound hands behind me remind me that whatever else happens, time to think and grieve and understand will not.

Once we come up into the zoo we're processed by the team on hand.

The pair of banshees on watch will have seen us coming. Sometimes more than a pair is assigned, sometimes even management, but always at least two. The idea being they can keep tabs on each other, so it's not just one remembering the information and passing it up the line. Making us work in teams never seems to work the way they want it to. We're all short-handed now and, even with us coming in late, there's only a pair from B-Troop, Saoirse and Yen, opening the gate to us one at a time, and it is strange to be let in first as leader.

These two are the last fucking thing we need.

Saoirse holds up a hand to ask the questions.

'Anyone sick?'

'Hah? No, nobody bit.' I'm confused. We're let in first usually, then the questions.

'Nobody bit?'

'She just said nobody bit,' Agata says. She's in pain

149

and exhausted, and she's had run-ins with B-Troop before, Saoirse especially.

'Nobody got the shits, no throwing up?' Yen asks me. This pauses me.

'No,' I say, and push my way through. Whatever plans I'd had of keeping the few bits I had stashed around me for trade in the zoo are fading. The toothbrushes and soap I want to keep are hidden so well nobody will find them.

We push our way through and are called forwards one by one and checked off as we hand over our weapons and packs and are patted down. The weapons will be brought by runners to management till they're needed again. Till we're needed again.

We – I, now – report our numbers, and we'll be got ready for our skin to be gone over for breaks. When we're naked we're let bathe, and then we can dress and eat. Then it's time to debrief, usually to the house mother, often the next day, depending what time it is when we land back in.

It smells, and there's too much to look at and try to take in, and I'm thinking about when we'll be given water and when fed, and I'm worrying about the debrief. Telling the lies about our leader, holding firm to them. Agata is already looking at me, reassuring, knowing what I'm thinking. She'll be beside me.

'Is that – is that Mare?' We all hear the whispers start up.

Mare is the last one in, shoved along by Lin. I watch her come over that final threshold, thinking about little Jay, what it must have been like for her, leaving the city for the first time. She must have been so frightened, coming out the walls with us. Trusting us.

We're all in, the way down to the tunnel barricaded again, the banshees standing guard. There's a sense of loneliness now amongst us all that we're back, a sense of sadness, a feeling that whatever thing we had to look forward to is gone and may not come again.

Still we are thirsty, but we'll sleep in safety tonight.

I glance at Mare.

Most of us will.

Eyes from all over watch us carefully; eyes on me, leading.

Management

MANAGEMENT IS SET UP IN A COUPLE OF LARGE houses with walled grounds on the north-west side of the city. They call them Government Buildings, and they're only a click or so away from the banshee trail and maybe two from the banshee blocks.

A walk away, but it might as well be another time and place. Here there are trees still, and ground not given away to growing crops. It's pretty. You could close your eyes some day when the wind was up, carrying away the smell of shit and the noise of people all trying to be quiet, and you could imagine you weren't in the city at all. Must be nice, having that right outside the window. People starving and freezing to death beyond.

We move through the city and it is quiet. The sun is setting. I stop us at the first gate and murmur to the old fella there with a long beard and flesh-flakes so bad I could see it twenty paces away. He hardly looks at me before he nods to the other man, a boy nearly, and the boy opens the gates for us, his bare feet slipping in the mud.

The building ahead of us, management headquarters, is tall and long with a grand porch at the front. The runner leads us off around to the side, and as we walk we can smell the leaves crumbling beneath our feet, we can feel grass. It's so wholesome, so pleasant, to get this breath of freshness in the city. Here, though, it is mixed with dread and discomfort. My first time at Government Buildings and I would prefer to be going into battle.

We're met at a second gate and, with hardly a word, Mare, bound and gagged still, is taken off us. Not the first time a banshee has been reported on and brought in by her troop. She's taken off in one direction and we are led in the other, around the back and down some steps and through a basement door. It's dark and it's hard to see after the good light of the day. We try anyway not to look in the doors left open to the rooms spread out along the corridor. There's a smell in here of something dark.

Other banshees have whispered about seeing things

through those doors, of women chained. I never saw those chains but I know banshees who've had 'missions' to get women from the shanties and bring them up. The men in this building can do what they like to anyone in the city, and they do it. The abuses are personal and individual down here in the basement. The further up you go, the more wide-ranging they get.

We go upstairs, and more stairs, the house unfolding itself to us in layer. It's not unlike banshee quarters, with smooth carved banisters and the windows, and the art on the walls, dark but intact, and the paint mostly gone in places but the whole place still together, but much more grand, much more intact. It's tall but even I can tell climbing up it, it's solid as a rock. This place isn't falling down on top of anyone's head for a long time, so it isn't. It should be safe here.

We follow the boy up on to the fourth floor. We walk through a large, cold room in which men, maybe twenty or so, stop whatever the fuck it is they're at to stare at us across the quiet gloom. I try to walk with the same swagger I do outside the city walls, chin lifted, eyes straight ahead. I pretend to be a leader.

I'm afraid in this room in a way I'm never afraid outside these walls. The skrake would never do to you some of things men will or want to, and that's the truth. And here, in this city, they do it and do it and do it.

For all their best efforts at keeping us separate and quiet, whispers travel between walls. They cannot tell us we do not see what we witness with our own eyes, nor deny the stories our scars tell. We see each other and we believe each other.

I lift my chin a notch higher.

The boy who led us this far has gone on through the door at the front of this room and left it ajar so I can see him talk to the man in there, the man leading the city now, in the same room as the last man who took over as leader. Who is, we'd assume, dead now. What becomes of ousted leaders is never made very clear in this city. We all know already, I suppose. The news that whatever new leader has set himself above us is a killer is not news.

My eyes accustom to the bad light and I see it there, on a table, our hard-won packs, a man's hands all over our stuff. I make straight for it, looking at it all spilling out over a wooden table. I stare at our lost riches while the boy opens another door, something is said very quietly, and we are ushered in.

I want to let my eyes wander all over the office but with the roomful of men behind us, staring at our backs through the open double doors, I feel too hemmed in to try and relax. We've practised this. The banshees briefed me on how these reports go.

On his desk is a full glass of clear water. I lick my lips, then wrest my eyes away to square my shoulders and look at him directly. My palms are sweating; there's prickling in my armpits.

Without looking up from his table he says, 'Just the leader.'

Nobody moves and I realise, with a shock of humility, that the banshees are waiting for my say so. Or pretending to, at the least.

I turn my head slightly and nod. Behind me, my banshees move out, and I square myself to face Boyle. The door closes and the atmosphere of the room changes so thoroughly I feel my ears pop. My heart is in my mouth and I feel close to fainting: with the banshees here I think I could hold it together because I have to. On my own, things are different.

'Sit,' Boyle says, though he is still standing behind his desk, looking down at whatever is on it with a frown.

Steeling myself, I step forwards and put the bottle I saved from my bag in front of him. Boyle pauses; his expression clears and he looks up at me. For the first time our eyes meet.

His head is entirely bald, his skin pale and shining. Brown, nondescript eyes: defined, oddly thick lips. He's not particularly tall but gives a feeling of solidity, like he'd be hard to move in one direction or another unless he'd decided to get there himself.

There's only one thing we want off him and just as well. We'd hardly be able to stop him.

'Orpen,' he says, the corners of his mouth moving up a little. 'Good. I understand you came back –' and this is the tricky bit I've been waiting for, terrible talk of a bright, strong little girl lost, '– with good supplies from the warehouses to the north.'

I say nothing, trying not to let on that the wind has been knocked out of me a little. I think about the way he's phrased this, as if the city had warehouses stocked around its perimeters for just the likes of us to go fetching. As if we didn't risk our lives for the bottle on his desk, as if we didn't lose anything.

The silence goes on so long I can hear a ringing in my ears.

The man clears his throat, his eyebrows raised. 'We're very grateful,' he says, which I find surprising.

Boyle sits down to look at me. He's feeling me out, seeing what it is that's the problem, whether I am being a good girl in the office and just too awed by him to give him whatever reaction he thinks appropriate.

'Sit,' he says again, and this time I do, grateful to only have to pretend with the top half of my body that I'm not about to fall apart with the fear.

'Of course,' he says with a satisfied little sigh, 'strictly speaking, the team was not authorised to work that area,' he glances down at his desk at something written there, 'or even to overnight outside the city walls.'

'Yes, sir.' I look away, back at the window, and breathe. 'We lost someone on the mission, sir.'

'Yes,' Boyle says, interested. 'A trainee. It's among my priorities to get our fighting numbers back up and that means more banshees, well trained. Well. Some wastage is natural if she wasn't up to it.'

'Yes, sir,' I say, thinking of how brave Jay was, and my voice breaks on 'sir'.

'It must have been hard for you.' His smile has a surety to it, and I don't know whether he's one of the leaders in this city because of this look of efficient and unshockable pleasant equanimity, or whether he created this look because of the role he wanted. I do know that he doesn't give a shit about a girl having died.

'We have had our doubts about your predecessor for some time,' he says then, watching me carefully.

I blink in astonishment. I never doubted Mare led by the rules till the last. I'd have murdered her cheerfully several times over these last years for it.

'You are surprised.'

'Yes, sir.' I recover myself. 'We did not know until she began to speak of leaving, or of not coming back in to the city. If we had ever heard of her speaking that way before, we'd have reported her.' I pretend to be at a loss. 'I am very surprised, and disappointed.'

Boyle nods, his eyebrows raised, and shifts comfortably in his chair.

'Orpen, you've been settling in well to your duties these last years.' I stare back but do not answer. 'Were you also surprised by your promotion?'

'Yes,' I say truthfully. 'I was.'

'We expect great things of you. You'll go far if you're careful.' They all use the same words.

'Thank you, sir.'

'Tell me about Sene.'

'She didn't know, sir.' This we were expecting and I answer quickly. 'I think Sene has been more let down than anyone else by Mare.'

Boyle thumbs the bone of his thumb against the soft worn wood of his desk.

'Well. Herself and Mare were partnered for a long time; it shows a lack of insight, if not something more . . . sinister.' He is not looking at me; I'm not even sure he is talking to me. But then he smiles his smile and he looks at me again. 'On the other hand, we would like to give her the benefit of the doubt. There are few enough banshees working. I will trust you,' he says, 'to keep a good eye on her.'

'Yes, sir.'

'Any further issues with your troop will land firmly at your feet. You understand?'

'Yes, sir.'

'No more surprises, Orpen.'

Now that he's got or has not got out of me whatever he was looking for, Boyle turns his eyes back to the papers on the desk. Even I can understand this means we are finished. I had thought that debriefs would be more detailed. An inventory of what was seen, what could be collected, how to prepare a team to get safely to the same area. There's something I have to get a better sense of before I leave the room.

'Sir?'

'Yes?'

'What will become of her?' I need to be sure.

'Are you going to argue for mercy?' He's amused.

'No, sir. I think she should be punished.'

Boyle outright smiles at me now and leans back in his chair. 'A night spent without permission beyond the walls. A trainee lost. These things might have been overlooked for long service. But your report of her wishing to leave – well, we know what we must do with traitors to the city. If people want to leave we must show them how to go.'

'When, sir?'

'Keen, eh?' He looks at me, narrowing his eyes slightly as if trying to see straight into me. 'Justice is swift in this city, girl.'

I have nothing to say to that.

'You've been very useful, Orpen. Stay the course and you'll go far.' He looks at me once more as I get up. 'You and your team may each pick from the goods you brought in.'

I nod and say thank you, but Boyle is already engrossed in whatever else it is he does. In that moment I think that he won't remember me till he needs me next.

As soon as I'm out of the room I second-guess everything. Does he know? He must be better than he seems at reading people . . . but perhaps it's never crossed his mind before to have to know how to read a woman.

I let myself walk fast, moving quickly past the stares of the men. My troop wait for me down the corridor. They file in behind me and down we go to the cool, evil-smelling basement and then up and out once more into the trees. We are quiet; we'll stay quiet till we get back to the dorm. I know what each of us is thinking, more or less. Lin is fuming, Agata is plotting. Aoife is still pure devastated, and Sene too, though Sene worries for Mare even more than the rest of us. I'm just frightened.

We walk quickly now, our tongues thick in our mouths. Nowhere to go except a cold brick box. Nothing to look forward to but silence, exile and cunning. And after exile, maybe freedom.

Two days, I figure. Maybe less.

It does not take long after my meeting with Boyle for a runner to come and find me.

I'm sitting in our training square, getting as much boiled water as I can into me, the sun on my back. When I feel a hand on my shoulder I jump, too well trained to scream, but in that moment I see it all: Boyle has changed his mind or found out something. They broke Mare, they know they know they *know*. I'll be taken now to Government Buildings, to the cellars, and after whatever happens there is over, the whole city will murder me. Whatever hopes I had for a free future dead. I wished I'd my knife safely tucked away, so I could do what I need to.

When I turn it's just a girl, nodding towards the top windows of the headquarters and that's how I know Ash wants to see me. I'm grateful for the cool of the inside of the building, the flights and flights of stairs in which my terrified heartbeat can slow. I take the steps one at a time, and once I arrive at the big wooden door, Ash herself opens it and accepts me in with a hug.

'A greenun lost.' She takes me by the shoulders and has a good careful look at my face to see am I OK, and I begin to cry with the kindness of it. She takes me into her arms again. 'I'm so sorry.'

I get myself under a kind of control and we sit on her couch together and she makes me go through the mission with her, nodding at certain points, making sure I have good clean water beside me, reaching for my hand when I describe little Jay being unable to get back up the ropes.

'I know it's hard. I loved Jay. I knew her since she came here, when she was no more than five or six. But even without being injured she'd have struggled.' She sighs. 'It's not my place to question management decisions, and I know how important it is – I more than anyone – to get our fighting numbers up. Everything is needed: more farmers, better wallers, more banshees. More breeders too, of course. But wastage happens no matter how promising the youth, how experienced the warrior.'

There's a long silence which I'm not up to filling. Ash squeezes my hand again and I murmur, 'You're so kind,' and I think I mean it.

'And now, head of the troop. That's hard too, in its way. We all admired Mare.'

She stands, our conversation over too quickly. I want to stay.

Ash walks me back down two flights of stairs. She greets any banshees, runners or other jobswomen we

163

meet warmly by name, and they step aside and lower their heads in respect or awe. There's such *power* to her. I feel important just clunking along in her wake.

Ash stops in front of a door towards the end of a dark corridor, opens it and gestures for me to step on through.

Inside, the room is a small rectangle with one large window; there's a metal bed to one side, shelves, a bowl and cup, a stool. Bedclothes.

Riches.

'You may not be aware, since your predecessor chose to sleep with the rest of the troop,' Ash says, going to the window and blowing on one of the panes of glass to clear it of dust. 'Every troop leader has privileges. As well as responsibilities.'

She sighs and turns to look at me. Holding her eye contact is at once difficult and inevitable. 'Management like you,' she smiles. 'And as we know, management are always right.'

I'm not sure if she's winking at me in the half-light.

'You could do very well. Just a few years in and you've your own room.' She passes close to me and reaches one hand out to squeeze my arm gently. 'Enjoy. You deserve it, I'm sure.'

The door closes softly behind her.

I'm alone with a closed door between me and the world for the first time in six years. I sit on the bed and fold my hands in my lap. It is only once I'm left alone do I notice she left a book for me on the shelf. I pick it up and inhale the good smell of the pages.

Punishment

MANAGEMENT MEET IN THE EVENING AND INTO the night because that is when they have always met. It suits them to gather together after they've got the business of the morning out of the way, lunched and rested.

You'd think they might change their habits, find better times to move around, start working in groups. They're secretive, shifty, unable to countenance being powerless, even as the evidence builds up around them in their shuffling, incapacitated colleagues.

They're ready to sit comfortably into the remains of the day. The children in the street know there'll be a punishment soon, another banshee, and so – a meeting of the men. With the nights drawing in there's only a few hours of light between this meeting and darkness. All of the women in the city know this, and the girls too.

And some of the women and the girls are emboldened. Passing beneath notice, watching and whispering together are their strengths, proven again.

Their little missions have been effective and they're confident now, though there are more of them, and they are being less careful. But management have always been careless in meeting all together, only a handful of watch-ful banshees between their gathering-places.

Two teams of two now, because they have seen it work. Three if they can get them, but the spare teams staying well clear. Each one armed with something she has found and sharpened and hidden away and sharpened again. There isn't a woman in the city now who doesn't arm herself, and some of the men watching now – farmers, wallers – learning, wondering.

The higher-ups live in that self-same building in which they meet: safely at the top and on the lower levels, but the lower-downs must go to their quarters in other buildings, in the dark if the meeting runs long at this time of year, which they do, and here the women seek their opportunity.

More men will be found dropped in the morning.

Room

I SIT IN MY ROOM, ALONE, THINKING.

Since we came back to the city, since I came back from my conversation with Boyle, I've become almost incapacitated by fear. And since my debrief with Ash, I understand better about obeying. I want to do it; it seems safer. Perhaps Boyle is different from the others, maybe he'll find a way to quell the plague, to up our numbers, to find a way for us all to live. And everything I fear for myself right now, every moment I expect B-Troop to appear and take me away screaming, to be punished, is what Mare is going through right now. I try not let myself feel that, moment by moment, and every moment I fail.

I couldn't do the will of others even if I'd wanted to

when I first came. Putting one foot in front of the other was more than I could manage, and then only with the help of Agata. Then I began to observe and finally I understood. If I obey, if I agree to live my life and order my priorities with those of our city leaders, if I can show that I am good at this, and ensure they notice my being good, then they will tempt me with greater and greater comforts. I will still be bound to these rules as I succeed, and they can change the rules at any time, but within certain confines, I will be rewarded. I'll be nodded to in hallways, I'll be spoken to by those we all admire. I'll rise in the system and, almost, become one of them. As long as I abide by whatever shifting, unspoken laws there are as well as those laid down in the punishment square. Unless luck or popularity turn against me.

I dig within myself to try and see whether I should give up my own thoughts. If I obeyed, if I went to Boyle with a plot like this . . . I'd get more than a room. A whole apartment, even, like Ash's.

I'd hoped when I came in these walls years ago that it'd be an end to having to find my own way. I hoped that in here someone would find it for me, the way a mother would. If that was ever true it isn't now.

Everything is more manageable once I'm moving. As soon as it's dark I pull my new clothes around me and I go out towards the latrines. There's nobody around. I veer left along stone walls, count ten paces from the corner, and dig. It's still there, buried not too deep, wrapped in my own precious socks. The knife that was put into my hands wet with banshee blood.

Inside again, I nod to a runner, tell her to fetch the troop to my room. I do it as if it's done every day – as far as I know it is not, but better to be open about it and caught and thought an idiot and too fresh a leader than trying to sneak four banshees into my room, even at night. If Ash knows or finds out, she'll forgive me.

I hide the knife before they come in. I still haven't said a thing about what happened at the end of the plinth at the last punishment. I wouldn't know how to put it into words.

Agata knocks quietly. She comes to me and puts her arms around me straight away. It feels good; she smells good. We don't usually spend a lot of time away from each other. The others follow on and they settle, three on the bed, Sene on the stool, her head in her hands. Lin stretched out on the floor.

'It went fine,' I tell them.

'About Jay.' Even in a whisper you can tell Aoife's upset, annoyed with everyone in the room.

Lin runs her hands through her hair.

'It wasn't a problem,' I say flatly. 'Natural wastage.'

Aoife nods, and even in the gloom as she lets her head

drop to her chest I see her nose dripping, her shoulders give a shaking heave. Lin reaches up for her and they hold hands.

We'll need someone to match with Sene now that Mare is gone. Banshees always work in pairs. It's how the whole system got started, they say. Women being told not to walk alone. Women watching out for women. Our predecessors, the women who came before us, they took it to heart, so they did.

I glance at Agata before I go on. 'He said to keep an eye out, for you especially, Sene.'

Sene nods, face stony.

'If anything went wrong, any of these missions, they'd have taken Mare,' Agata says. Where she hears such things I don't know, but we all believe her. 'They were just waiting.'

I nod. 'He said they were watching her.' It's my job now to do a lot of things, but backing up Agata, and her backing up me, is always my first. 'They weren't surprised, he said.'

'Be better if I'd gone with her,' Sene says, rubbing her nose with the back of her hand. 'Two of us up there would have been better.'

'I'll be up there with her,' I tell her.

'Better one of you injured instead of both,' Agata says. 'We all agreed, Mare especially. Besides, they'd have mistrusted the whole troop. He could have put us all up there for punishment. We were lucky.'

'Doesn't feel lucky,' Sene says.

'At least they really believe we're with them,' Lin says, and I wonder if it's true.

Another sniffle from Aoife.

'Get it out of your system now,' Lin says towards Aoife, if not to her, exactly. 'You know they don't like to see us having feelings.'

'The punishment won't happen tomorrow is about all I know,' I say. 'This may be the only time we all have together again to talk free—'

I shut up and we all stiffen at a noise outside the door. We hardly breathe for a few moments, listening. I wait till I'm happy enough it was nothing before I go on.

'You know you don't have to sleep here,' Lin says suddenly, and too loud. I wonder should I try and remind her who is leading here, but she knows well. 'Mare never used to.' She spits out the words. She's upset because Aoife is upset, I'm guessing.

'We need to go over our plans,' Agata says gently. 'This is the best place for that.'

'We have tomorrow: we probably only have tomorrow.' I focus, trying to ignore the prickling in my armpits. 'Let's go over it again. We need to gather as many people together as possible. Mare has taken care of that.'

I'm not keen to linger on that detail. 'Once we're up there, Boyle will call me forward.'

'We think,' Lin says.

'He will,' I say, my voice coming out more confident than I feel. 'Then it'll happen fast. Management won't have time to react.'

I don't want to think too hard about my role in what happens there either. 'So it goes to plan, we're up there, and we get to ask the question.'

I imagine it, my being up there, asking people to trust me, to come with me. The blood not cleaned off my hands yet. There's not one bit of anything I have to do here that I like.

'OK, let's move on,' Agata picks it up. 'We tell everyone to gather, we meet them by the tunnel. We go out like usual. They'll know to be quiet. We head west.' She takes a deep breath. 'It'll work because it's simple.'

'We need more prep,' I say, shaking my head. 'We've got to survive on the road for three days, maybe more. Probably skrake will be on us.' I think about that and then go on, 'Skrake will be on us, maybe a lot of them. We need at least some people to know, so they can bring food, water, medical supplies. We need strong people to carry whoever can't walk.'

I close my eyes and listen to the silence lengthen. When I open them, though, Sene is nodding. 'She's right. We need to guess who we can trust here, other than each other.'

There's another long silence before what I hope and think will happen happens.

'I know a waller,' Aoife says.

Agata laughs a light, quiet laugh. 'Oh, yeah.'

'He's trustworthy,' Lin says, and the way Aoife looks at Lin after she says this is like the light coming out behind a cloud. It's like love.

'OK,' I say. 'See if your friend knows anyone who'll want to get ready, who can carry. Those wallers, they're strong.'

Lin's not finished. 'I know someone in farming too. We can go tomorrow.'

'You trust them?' I ask.

'Fuck off, Orpen,' Lin says.

'Who else?'

'I want to talk to the breeders,' Agata says.

I nod. 'Anybody know anyone else?'

'Place isn't exactly designed for it,' Sene mutters. 'Anybody know anyone in the shanties?'

I think of that woman whose home we tore apart. I think of her child.

'Management, the rest of the banshees – I don't think we can ask, even. They'll have to decide right then whether they're with us or not.'

I pause. I have to ask. 'What about Ash?'

They all turn to look at me. 'What about her?' Sene says.

'She's practically management, Orpen,' Agata says impatiently, and I know she's right, but I want to tell her to fuck off at the same time.

'There's kindness in there,' I say, shrugging my shoulders a little.

'OK, any more ideas?' Agata asks.

'Weapons?' Lin asks.

Agata shakes her head. 'Under management control. Trying to get in is too risky. If we're lucky a few of them will be with us. We'll only have whatever we've pilfered.'

Sharpened bits of metal – deadly enough, but not much good for throwing. Nothing bigger than a few inches.

'We only need ourselves,' I say, wondering if it's true.

I want them all to go so I can stop pretending here.

'What about me?' Sene says. I'd never have thought I'd hear her sound forlorn. I didn't know she had feelings like that in her.

'Stay at barracks tomorrow,' I say. 'Out of sight. Let's not prompt people to go second-guessing your loyalty. Stay in here if you can.'

I can make out Sene's bulk in the darkness. I can just see her putting her head back in her hands. The last thing she needs is a whole day of imagining what's going to happen to Mare. What's happening right now, right this minute.

I think she's done, but Sene says one more thing. 'Nobody's going to catch and punish me after all this kicks off.'

I can feel Agata nodding beside me.

'Sene's right. Let none of us be caught. It'd be worse than death.'

'We know,' Lin says. Her fright is making her angrier than usual even.

'Gather supplies wherever you see an opportunity. Food, weapons,' Agata says.

'Tools,' I add. 'Containers.'

The troop, what's left of it, nods.

'Keep it simple, keep it focused,' Agata says. 'Don't talk to anyone you don't have to.'

'If everything goes to shit, get out however you can. Go west. Save who you can,' I go on. It sounds a bit grim. 'Couple of days and we'll be out, or we won't,' I smile. I want to have the last word and I want it to be as encouraging as we deserve.

'We should burn the whole place. Let Z in, close the gates on them.' Lin.

There's silence till I glance at Sene, who looks back at me, and I realise this is mine to deal with.

'There's good people here still.'

'No,' she says again. 'If you stay here it means you're OK with everything that happens.'

'*We*'ve been OK with everything that's happened,' I point out, though it's not true, exactly. 'We were all at it, doing what we were told. We'll be at it again tomorrow.'

'We haven't been fine about this in a long time,' Aoife says, looking up at me at last. I nearly flinch at her eyes, narrowed in anger.

'Yeah, you should have trusted me a lot earlier,' I say back to her, stung.

Silence again and this time I don't try to have the last word. Instead the quietest of us takes it.

'People are frightened, Lin,' I say in the end. 'They're trying to survive, same as everyone else, same as us.'

There's a pause and I try a different tack.

'At least there's a pretty good chance we'll kill Boyle,' I say, and the others nod along.

'Shoulda never come back through these gates,' Sene says.

'This is the plan,' Agata says. Resourceful, determined Agata.

Nobody disagrees but everyone gets up to leave, filing out silently ahead of Agata. At the door, she surprises me by closing it and turning to me.

She looks at me for a long moment and then whispers, 'Can I stay here tonight?'

I nod without giving it a moment's thought. I'm glad. I want this distance between us gone. I want to feel the way I felt back in the tunnel, when it was just the two of us. And a flesh-eating monster trying to devour us alive. I open my mouth to say so but she beats me to it.

'Tell me again about the island.'

The Shanties

'O RPEN!'

I haven't slept like that in – in years, so out, completely asleep. As if when I closed the door the world disappeared: as if I were safe.

Nobody should sleep like that.

I remember where I am and get up quickly, go to lift out my one good knife, the knife that was given me, from the wall where I've been practising throwing it, getting used to the weight. I'm getting better; I'm nearly there. I hide it again and I open the door.

Outside, a runner: a girl, about the same age as Jay. The age Jay was.

'You're wanted.'

I nod. 'Get Agata.' It's only when I say her name that I remember she stayed with me last night, the two of us passed out on the little bed.

She's not here now and I didn't hear her leaving. She could have been gone half the night.

The runner is gone. I close my eyes and rub them, and remember I've water right here to splash on my face. I swill a mouthful, swallow it. The luxury. I've a tooth-brush, soap.

The light in the room is sludgy but dawn is long broke. A new day.

I go out and there she is, waiting for me by the stairs. I glance at her but it's hard to read her face in the gloom. Wordless, we go together up the stairs.

Ash's apartment is bright and warm as usual, the fire in its little grate. Where does she get the fuel?

'Good,' Ash says. 'Nice to see you again so soon, Orpen.' I can feel Agata look at me.

Ash sits behind her table, the way Boyle or one of them would. The remains of a meal strewn across it. 'Thank you for coming so promptly. There has been another attack.' She speaks quick and quiet: she is quite sure of being heard. We strain in case we miss a word. 'A man, struck down and left injured by a gang when walking back to his quarters.'

We are peace-keepers, I remind myself. That's all

this is – they don't know anything.

'Did he get a look?' Agata asks.

'No, it was dark and it happened quickly. They were women. At least two.'

'Not banshees,' Agata says as if she can't believe it.

Ash looks at her closely. 'A team working together closely. You can imagine the conclusions people draw from this information.'

'They had weapons?' I ask.

'Something sharp.'

A jag of glass or metal with a handle made out of fabric, some bit of plastic found and melted, a sharpened stick. You can stab someone with nearly anything if you're keen enough on the idea.

'His injuries were . . . intentional,' says Ash in her calm, rich voice.

'What do you mean?' I ask. Of course they intended to injure him: probably they thought they had killed him.

'He was cut very deliberately to ensure he wouldn't walk well.'

A silence as I realise what we're dealing with. The men being hobbled around the city. They must know now that those banshees they threw over the wall at the last punishment, it wasn't them. I don't stop to wonder if management feel guilty about torturing and murdering two innocent women.

'Why him?' I ask.

Ash raises an eyebrow.

'Presumably he was just . . . in the wrong place, at the wrong time?' Agata puts in.

'What was he wearing?' I ask. 'They might have been after the cloth only. Did they say anything to him?' I ask.

'No,' Ash says.

'Can you tell us anything else?' I ask, after a moment.

Ash considers a moment. 'This isn't the first. It's been happening, on and off, for some time.' We know this already. I've seen the men, being helped around the city. 'Always management, always a man walking home at night.'

'Where are they coming from?' I ask innocently. Men wandering around on their own at night can't be up to any good.

Ash pretends not to hear. 'Always two women. Well, two people, actually, and one is a woman. We've been assuming the other is too.'

Agata, beside me, feels unsurprised as ever.

'The same two?' I feel I should ask something, see can we get anything else out of her. I just don't know where we'd start looking.

She shrugs. 'Impossible to know. Seems very likely. But possibly there's more than one team.'

She's watching us very closely, I realise.

'That's why those two women were punished,' I say, as if it's just dawning on me. There's silence for a moment and then I add, because I want it said out loud, 'This means they were innocent.'

'Not necessarily,' Ash counters. 'Well, the men are stripped as part of the attack and this morning they found fabric belonging to this man in the zoo.'

It strikes me only then that she's annoyed with us, with her favourite troop, for harbouring a traitor like Mare. She's annoyed with herself for not seeing it, for not knowing. This run to the zoo is a little exercise for us, to see how vicious we'll be for her, to see if we're keen to prove ourselves.

'You don't think it was people from the shanties?' I say quickly, as if I can cover up my thoughts.

'No,' Ash says airily. 'But isn't it obvious what you've to do?' she says, and I know this is the end of the conversation now. 'Management will expect results quickly.'

Sene, Aoife and Lin wait for us outside. We leave the barracks and head towards the zoo together.

'That was good timing,' Lin says, her voice flat, and I glance at Agata. Her face is blank and she pretends not to notice all of us looking at her till she meets my eye.

'What?' She laughs. 'You think I somehow planned for two women to go attack some management arsehole last night so we'd be sent off on a little adventure?'

'That's literally what we're all thinking,' Aoife says.

'Yeah,' Lin says.

'Me, too,' Sene joins in.

They look to me.

'Sorry, yeah,' I say. I'm wondering, for all I know her, how well do I know her?

'It's just, we all *know* you,' Aoife says.

'Anyway, I was with Orpen all last night,' Agata says smiling, airily.

There's a course of 'Wooooos' and an 'at last' from Aoife.

I shush them and we run on, saying nothing about Agata's being gone when I woke up. She knew I'd say nothing. I look over at her but her face is immutable as ever. She's picked up that length of tubing she found at the airport and is carrying it awkwardly over her shoulder. More secrets, I think.

'You should let us in on these things,' Lin says, echoing my thought.

I think again of the two dead banshees. I think of Mare.

'I'd heard about these women going after management,' Agata says. 'We've all seen these men up towards management, limping around. Look, there goes one now,' and we all turn to see a tall man stooping along painfully, another man helping him. 'There's a good few of them now. That's all I know. Banshees don't need much of an excuse to go kicking around the shanties anyway.'

'How many is a good few?'

'I've seen about a dozen,' Aoife says. 'Been keeping an eye out for them. Mal says—'

'Who's Mal?'

'Her boyfriend,' Lin says to me quietly, rolling her eyes.

'Mal says it's what took down the last leader, the one before Boyle. That he couldn't stop it.'

We're chatting too much and I glance around to see if anyone has noticed. People are going about their business, working hard not to make eye contact as we jog by. The others are silent and I think everyone's mind has started to drift to other things, but Agata breaks it.

'All right! I'd heard some of the victim's clothes had ended up in the shanties, I got one of the runners to put it in her ear.'

A guffaw from Lin.

'We've all our work for the day, we should get on with it.'

Generally, being outside your barracks or whatever space that is meant for you, is forbidden. Banshees will stop you and ask you questions and send you back with a few slaps for yourself. I have done that myself. It's a part of the job we do here, part of what we're fed for. Banshees won't usually challenge other troops, though.

I feel shy in front the others, walking first, giving orders, if there are any to be given, as if my leadership is not real – which it isn't. Even still, I would like someone to try to stop us today. I would like to flex the new looseness off my constraints and feel even the narrowness of my new power. Instead, today, people seem to go out of their way to avoid us. There'll be time enough to work this recklessness out of my shoulders, plenty of places I can put my itching knuckles.

On the gates of our own small barracks' boundaries are Shiv, who I know, and some fresh-looking girl I don't. Shiv nods and steps aside, hardly looking at us. We won't be popular with any banshees on the make just now with our leader about to be punished.

There are men going about their business already, farmers and skivs mostly. We walk quickly, trying not to look about us too focused. I glance at Agata, who has that careful, slightly bored, blank expression on her face. I arrange my own features the same way, best I can, and feel comfort in the light steps of the three friends behind us.

A good stretch from banshee blocks to the shanties,

but we've been running and I've been thinking about the city rather than what's ahead of us and that's a good thing.

We get to the gates and slow to a walk.

As we move, we see nobody. People are hiding away, keeping quieter even than usual, a path of solitude opening up before us.

My eyes are wide for that woman with the scar and her child. I hope she's hidden well from us but I want to see her. I want to know if she's OK.

I used to think ending up in the shanties was the worst fate: no surety, no rations, the whole of the city looking down at you. There's more freedom here, though, if you can eke a living. I am beginning to think different, about law and about freedom. Or – I am beginning to see the way I grew up as being closer to this independent way in the shanties than our way up in the city.

We'll have been seen before we reached the gates even. Word will have got out by whatever mechanisms they have. They'll be hiding the children, I hope.

Something big they must have had in here once, the way the walls around the zoo are built. We get past the concrete structures and over the central marsh. We're watched carefully by many, and followed by a small group of youngsters. Before long we're stepping over wires holding tarp in place, around sheet metal and crumbling bricks. In the morning light I glimpse what is inside people's dwellings, and look away again. Those intimacies are not meant for the likes of us, with our meals given us every day. I check my features again and try to make sure they're blank but hard.

I feel frightened and I almost want someone to challenge us so we can kick things off as a response, rather than it coming from nowhere. Someone's going to get beat up. I want it to be someone who can take it.

I wear: the same shirt I've worn most of these last six years, the fabric shiny, patched on the elbows and along one seam at the side, more grey now than black; two coverings over it of lightweight cloth to guard against cold and wet, wrapped around myself and tied at the back. Trousers, black, ill-fitting, filched from a corpse, a skeleton really, back when missions were more common; shoes, light, the toes cut off as they're too small, dark in colour, and wraps, of course, with packing behind them, always, black. None of it mine. Taken from bodies, to be taken from my own body when that time comes.

I've better clothes from the airport, worn in through our checks and allowed back on me afterwards, stashed away now. Coming down here wearing riches would feel disrespectful.

Agata and the others are dressed a little different, but

essentially the same: dark, protected and mobile. Even if we were naked they'd know us for banshees. They'd know us for being the dirtied thumbs of management.

A man, nearly as broad as he is tall and that's rare, and according to Aoife, attractive, steps in front of me. He stares down at me, his legs planted solidly in the mud, wide apart. That's his first mistake, I think, but I do not take the advantage of it. His eyes move to the length of pipe Agata is gripping.

There're fights in the city, quiet, desperate heaves over rations and belongings, but they're quelled fast, one way or another. We do our work well; there's many that enjoy it.

Because he knows that I can kill him I stay quiet until his friend says, 'What's your business?'

I don't take my eyes off this flesh-brick in front of me and he doesn't blink either, so I smile. When he draws himself up to his full height I laugh outright. Then I glance back and give a nod, and at this Sene, Aoife and Lin begin to work their way through the area, shoving, intimidating. Whatever dwellings they can get into, they'll turn upside down.

While they work, I raise my voice to tell everyone that has gathered, 'A man was attacked in the city last night.' Usually Agata would do the talking as my second. I'm trying to practise, though. 'We have been sent to—'

'Find someone to make an example of?'

Flesh-brick and his pal Boulder step forward again like they're trying to make a wall, their eyes on the work that banshees are continuing to do behind us. It's still quiet. Other than these two, the shanty-dwellers aren't putting up a word of protest. They stand, staring. I much prefer the way these two men have of trying to deal with us.

I let my banshees do their work, trying to look like I'm not interested in the crowd, pretending I'm not searching their faces for the woman and her little girl. I'm not sure what I want from it exactly. To take them aside and tell them to get ready?

'There'll be a punishment,' I say. 'Everyone must attend.'

Breeders

I'M HUNGRY AND WANT TO GO BACK TO BARRACKS, REST, go again this afternoon. I want a minute to think. Nobody has thought hard enough about what might happen when people get to the island. If anybody survives that long.

I know from the way Agata is going that barracks is not where we're headed, though. She's that damn pipe with her, and other ideas. We work our way back out of shanty territory, Agata and me a few steps in front.

I'm tired. Half the day gone already.

We get moving, jogging north again on the main road towards the rest of the city.

At the turn-off, I give Sene, Aoife and Lin the nod, and we go northwards without them.

The breeders are housed in buildings that are nearly as good as management's, and better than the banshee barracks. They've private rooms, even the lowlier ones, and there's good care between them, and good rations. We never have the opportunity to go into their space. They're not meant to need the likes of us to keep them in line, I guess. They're either really good or there are other control methods.

In the time it takes to jog there, with Agata lugging her pipe beside me, I have grown nervous as well as embarrassed at myself. I'm not afraid of meeting breeders in the same way I am, or was, of meeting those people in the shanties.

I've never been here before and I don't know what to expect or how to act. Beside me, Agata's got this energy, and I know from the cut of her that she's been here before and she's glad to be going back.

At their boundaries they've no banshees standing. Men are meant to be let at them, I suppose.

The quiet here is different from the hush in the shanties. There, it's a riot of sheets of metal, dirtied tarps held in place with rocks and the feeling of being watched without being able to see faces. Here, there's nothing: they must all be kept inside or in their own private yard, just as we are. Nobody much coming or going.

The old building is grander even than management's, now that I see it up close, though smaller. The house curves out towards us in two bulbous swellings, and there are windows everywhere. Hard as it'd be to defend a place with so much glass, for a few clicks in most directions the place is pure flat. There's paths for walking and the rest is given over to the farmers. All these curves, even the building feels feminine, enticing somehow.

A few steps, overgrown with grass and weeds, up the rise of three feet to the place is the only slope to be found. No handy hill on which to mount a defence; no woods or brush or long grass in which to hide. The feeling of exposure in this place gives me chills.

Their good building is shabby, more than ours, even. Few of the windows have their glass intact; some are covered by boards. To the left, one part of the roof is sloping dangerously. You can see where the damp from the failed tiles and gutters runs down the rest of the structure. Altogether it looks nearly as if the building is winking sadly at you.

I prefer our dirty, upright dwelling, ugly and functional, largely intact.

Ahead of us, just a little away from the main building, sit three figures. One, then the second and third together, go running to the main building. Even the way they run is different. They look as if they are just playing at it. Feet and ankles bare.

I expect . . . I don't know what. Hostility, same as if we went in unannounced to the farmers, or they to us. The women here smile at us, though. Tired eyes and long hair.

We walk side by side straight up the open ground in front of the big house. After a moment, a group comes to greet us, four of them, with long hair, fabric arranged as dresses, clean hands held up to their faces so they can see us against the violent sun.

'Agata,' the tallest of them says. 'Outlier.' The tone is so friendly, towards both of us. Beside me, Agata reaches out her hand and the two women grasp each other's fingers for a moment.

'Beth,' Agata says, her voice warm.

'She's where you'd expect,' Beth says. The women with her smile at me and I smile back, the muscles feeling stiff, but Agata is on the move again, peeling leftwards. The energy coming off her is unsettling. We move together, but I'm following her again. I'm invisible to her, I feel, for the first time. I glance behind us and the three women are watching us and talking amongst themselves. Nice life they've here, I think, to be talking to each other so free under the sky. You wouldn't be getting laxness like that now in the barracks.

Around the back of the main house there are more buildings: sheds and lean-tos, a greenhouse, even, full of something growing tall and wild. By the smell I'd say the breeder latrines are not so far off. Behind them, squat buildings, and we go around these and towards a boundary wall.

Where did Agata learn this place? How does she know where to go?

From nowhere, a shape, running at us – small, quick and straight moving, not like a skrake and yet . . .

It hurls itself at Agata, and while I reach for a knife that is not there, she laughs, delighted.

A child, perhaps eight years old.

It takes a moment for reality to start back up on me. Half of me is fighting, killing this creature in front of me with as much brutality as I can muster; my hands shake a little with the effort of not using them, and I feel nearly nauseous with the climb-down back into the real moment. It takes a time before the world rights itself enough for me to pretend there's nothing wrong. I've to breathe through clenched teeth a while.

'Hello, little soldier,' Agata says, her smile so wide I can see all her back teeth. I never see her smile like this; I find it nearly ugly. From around us, more children are coming out, though most hang back together shyly.

Agata is not being quiet: she must feel sure of some safety, talking in the open air here.

'Orpen, this is Noah.'

Noah gives me a long look and says, 'Hello.'

'Noah, Orpen is a banshee like me,' Agata says, still smiling.

'I am,' I say uncertainly.

'I want to be a banshee when I grow up,' Noah says, wheeling off Agata and throwing some slight punches to the air. 'And fight the skrake and go outside the city and . . .'

Agata catches my eye, but don't I know already to keep my mouth shut?

'Shhh,' Agata tells Noah. 'You don't want to be getting in trouble now. Is Cat in the workshop?'

Noah is still busy throwing punches and kicks, but he pauses long enough to point a direction and we move towards a low brick building a little apart from the others.

'How many children are here?' I ask, looking over my shoulder at the small eyes watching us.

Agata shrugs. 'Always lots of mouths to feed.'

She doesn't want to answer questions, so I'm going to stop asking. I'm just going to watch and listen, a whole new sense of dread building within me. I try to shake out my arms, get ready for whatever's coming next.

I think of the way she looked at me, in the airport, the soft light on her skin.

'That's not the question you should be asking,' she tells me.

I blink and for a moment see how tired she is.

'What should I be asking?' I say more gently.

Before she can answer, the door is pulled back and something flies at Agata once more. I've only time to get my hands up before I recognise it's a woman, long white hair flowing. They kiss, long and slow and hard, eyes closed and hands everywhere.

I stand with my mouth open; I close it, look away, glance back again. Clear my throat.

They're still at it, glommed together.

The woman is older than I'd first thought, older that I'd expected anyone would be in this part of the city. Her throat is lined, her hands, brought tenderly up to Agata's face, are old hands.

I look away only to look back again.

You don't see people kissing in this city. I don't know have I ever seen it before, though I've heard it, I suppose. I take a step back and look away towards the other buildings; I want to give them privacy. You'll hear things all right if you happen to find yourself in a quiet corner of the banshee quarters. You might interrupt a couple of banshees, but I haven't seen women kissing like this, open and joyful, since Mam and Maeve. Long time ago and far away.

Even still and all, I do not know where to look. Figuring out where to look or where not to look is keeping me busy and I'm glad for that. I don't want to be feeling the feeling that is growing within me. Despair.

'Orpen,' laughs Agata. 'This is Cat.'

Cat smiles at me, her clear brown eyes looking at once happy and knowing. 'Hello,' she says warmly.

I nod silently.

'You were not joking,' Cat says to Agata. 'The pipe!'

'Right size?'

'Looks like it. At last! Come on.' Cat lifts the pipe Agata has been dragging half-way around the country and carries it into the building, and Agata steps after her.

'Come on,' she pauses to say, smiling at me. 'It's OK.'

The light is bad inside and I stand at the doorway blinking a few minutes to get a handle on things. It looks a little bigger inside than out; it is much cleaner than I'd have guessed, the floor swept and the surfaces clear of dust and dirt, no mean feat in the city in a dry spell.

Cat has taken the tubing to the furthest side of the room, Agata trailing her, talking about the airport and the mission. She's walking funny and I realise she's limping. All this time I thought it was carrying that damn pipe making her uneven, but of course, it's her leg, still, troubling her.

I feel unseen again. It's like coming up for air, even with the jolt of loneliness, and sadness, watching Agata without her watching me back. All this happiness in her and I never knew. I'd have bet my life that I was the closest person to her in the world. I think I have bet my life on that.

My eyes are adjusting to the dimness. I've never been in a room like this before. There are surfaces against each wall and a rickety table in the middle. Most of it is made from the kind of sheet metal you'd see in the shanties, held in place with wire and string, rocks and bricks. A plastic cup, rusted bits of metal, warped plastic. Junk mostly, even by the city's standards. Some bigger plastic bins and some good little lengths of tubing are the only things of value I can see. I pick things up and look at them and put them back down again, my hands sweaty and my heart hopeless, keeping an eye on where Agata and Cat are. I can tell from here that Agata is not being listened to. Agata is always heard amongst us.

'O,' Agata calls me. 'Come and see.'

At a workbench Cat is assembling several bits of rubbish, making tssk noises, letting things fall apart, bringing them together again.

'Well?'

'Maybe,' Cat says, distracted. She rubs the back of her hand against her forehead, pushing back some hair and leaving a long streak of grease, catching the light on her dark skin. 'Maybe, yes.'

Agata turns to look at me, grinning still.

'I think Cat may have solved our water problem.' Agata, laughing, wrestles Cat away from the tubes and sets her on a stool by the central table, facing me.

It takes time for me to understand what the fuck she's going on about.

'You said before there's an issue with the place you came from, with Slanbeg,' Agata is saying, but it's such an alien sensation, having that word uttered in this room in this city – the word that is my whole past. My whole self.

'Orpen? You said the source there was weak, yes?' Cat is brisk, flicking her great sheet of white hair behind one shoulder.

How can a problem with water supply on an island three days' walk from here be fixed in this place? I nod anyway, fuck it. 'Not as much rain as here, no rivers.' I look at Agata and she nods at me, encouraging. I sigh. 'There's a spring we'd get water from but it was sludgy, tough-going. And that was six years ago.'

Cat's looking at me intensely. 'But it's an island? In the city we've rain, and we've the part of the river that runs under the wall; it's not clean, but it's good enough for the crops. And we can boil it, stew it up with mash and it's safe enough to drink.'

'Most of the time,' Agata puts in, and Cat nods.

'Right. If it's treated it'd be perfectly safe, but we're dealing with workers who won't boil it long enough, dirty pots – any number of things can go wrong. But in a perfect system, boiling the water would make it safe enough to drink.'

'How do you know?' I ask. She speaks fast, like Aoife, but her tone is like Ash's, sure and deep.

'Now you can't boil sea water, that's no good,' Cat is saying, ignoring me, the lines on her face deepening for a minute, rubbing more grease into her forehead with the back of her hand. 'Here's what happens; the water boils off and you're left with salty residue. So it's a good way to get salt, I guess.'

'I know this already,' I say, pretending to be bored.

She doesn't hear me. 'And maybe there's enough of a source for even bad water to boil, if we can clear it – but maybe not. Maybe's not good enough. But then, I saw . . .'

She gets up from her seat and wanders around her work-place, picking up items and putting them down again. I look at Agata, who is staring at Cat open-mouthed, smiling slightly. The look is frightening to me. She's too unguarded.

Cat clatters through the piles of junk till she finds what she needs.

A book.

'Look,' she says, and she wipes her dirty hands on her legs at least before she starts to turn the pages.

'You can read?' I say drily.

This she hears.

'Right,' she rounds on me. 'Stupid breeders, good for nothing but saying yes to management and lying back and wiping up after the babies we are *forced* to—'

'Cat,' Agata says, putting a hand on her arm with infinite gentleness. Love in her voice. 'O, when you know Cat better, you'll see that she's one of the smartest people in existence. Even management see—'

'A little,' Cat breaks through her gritted teeth. 'I was one of the breeder generations told by management we weren't fit for it, but I learned a little, growing up. I can read a picture easy as anyone.'

The way she says the word 'management,' as if she found a sharp little rock in her mouth. The same way Agata says it, and I wonder who learned from who.

She holds out the pages to us and we peer down. The paper is damp-looking, barely holding together. The colours are worn out but you can make things out just the same. I can read but I can't make out what I'm meant to understand here.

'Look,' Cat says again, and points with one grubby finger. 'You put the seawater in this big barrel and you put it over a flame. The water heats and steam gathers here.' She points. 'And then as it travels along this tubing –' Here she stands and goes to fetch the big plastic pipe Agata foraged for her. 'It cools, turning into liquid again.'

Agata and myself exchange a glance.

'It's clean!' Cat says, nearly smiling. 'It'll be clean, drinkable water. You can just pick it up from here and drink it. We'll have salt too. Course, then we'll have a fuel problem.' She licks her lips. 'One thing at a time.'

'You're sure?' Agata asks her, glancing at me. 'People will die if we can't give them water, if we can't grow crops.'

'People are dying here,' says Cat. She shrugs, and the feeling of discomfort, of near-panic, takes another step forwards, up towards the top, within me.

'You've got to take a leap, sometimes,' she goes on. 'All you can do is offer a way out, and be honest, and hope that people take it. But this?' She tilts her chin towards the picture. 'This will work.'

Agata and I walk back towards our own square. I'm thinking of my room, of shutting the door and putting my arms around my knees and my head on to them and closing my eyes. I need to get away, to think, to see if I can calm down.

I don't want to cry in front of Agata. She'll only ask me why.

There's nobody much around and already I'm getting used to being able to walk around free like this. Now we're senior we've these privileges.

'It hasn't been going on that long,' she says to me, quietly, eventually.

There's nothing I want to say to her, but I'm thinking again about the attacks. There are lots of thoughts coming now, fast and loud. I knew she'd told other banshees my secrets, but telling someone outside our small sisterhood is worse again.

Running off to kiss some breeder in the middle of the night.

'You needed me to get the banshees OK with not just us leaving, because you wanted to bring Cat too,' I say at last. 'What else?'

When she stays quiet I go on: 'I don't keep secrets. Not from you, not for a long time. I trusted you with it all . . . with all my . . . *insides*,' I tell her, reaching for the right words. 'And you *used* it.'

I thought I was the most important thing to her, all this time. Now if I could hurt her, I would.

Room

I GO SLOWLY BACK TO BARRACKS, TRYING TO GET USED to the feeling of walking on my own and letting Agata limp off her own way. If everything goes to plan I'll be doing a lot more of it, and with that thought I feel a new surge of pure black unhappiness.

Back at barracks, Ash is training in the square. An odd thing: she has her pet skrake out with her, chained up carefully to one of the huge metal hoops fixed into the building. She must have got B-Troop to move it from her private garden. Just now, though, the skrake isn't being used. Ash is sparring with the other banshees. Nobody can resist stopping to watch.

Large, pale and beautiful, she seems languid until she's

opposite you with her delicate little fists raised. I watch as she performs a perfect scorpion kick. Her opponent never sees Ash's heel, coming or going, and is dropped in the dirt, falling almost gently, like a leaf. Ash never holds back on those rare occasions now she's in the yard. She's always trying to get us to go hard in sparring sessions, to fight as if we mean it. She turns around, grinning at her audience and as she looks she catches my eye and nods at me. It's hard not to smile back at her, even on a day like this. A last day.

I get to my room and close the door gratefully, leaning my forehead against the wood. I can't stop the thoughts from coming; how I never felt right or comfortable sleeping in dorms with the banshees, in beds warmed by the farts of someone else before we got into them. Part of the reason we've shorn hair is because of the lice, so they say. Banshees are dark and dirty. Breeders light, clean, loving. I look down at my hands, the black under the fingernails and grit driven hard into the lines on my palms.

Banshees never grew up with privacy. They mightn't be comfortable with it if they had it. This is what I tell myself. I grew up with my own place and space and pace, and clean sheets and a door that closed and locked, and plenty of time alone.

And now I have it.

I try again to imagine running west with Agata, the way my mother and her lover once did, and I can't. The thing I'd hardly let myself dream about is ruined.

There is a knock on the door.

'Yes?'

I palm my knife before the door opens. The shaggy head of a runner peers around it. 'Will I bring your dinner?'

'Yes.'

The door closes again.

Sitting on the bed again, I look about me and take stock. The small, rectangular room: the bed, a bucket so I needn't even suffer the latrines. The floorboards, cold and smooth. The window letting in the light, with its view over the training square. Shelves in one corner: I could put my toothbrush there, my clothes, some books maybe, if Ash keeps liking me. I'm up two flights already. I could climb higher.

The little twinge in my side. In the old days I'd have told Agata, the kind of thing a partner should know. And I should know how that nasty cut on her leg is doing, but here we are.

On the little stool beside the bed is a cup and a book, *A History of Dublin*, sent down to me. Ash'll call me, probably, and give me meat from somewhere and talk about the good comfortable life that is hers and could be mine. She'll tell me I can earn it through work and merit. She won't be wrong, not entirely wrong.

Meanwhile, the wallers work their dirty hands to the bone for half the rations I get a day. To go lie down in the mud at night, in rooms made of metal sheeting placed at right angles to the cold hard ground. But isn't there always someone suffering?

Below, though, in the dorms, the troop may be talking about me: I'll never be the leader Mare was.

I should go down to them, I should stay the course and suffer the dorms as Mare did – Mare, who I thought I knew but did not. Same as Agata.

Instead, I get up to check the softness of the wood the door is made of. Four paces to the window. I turn, grip my one knife, throw and catch by the handle and then aiming, throw again, putting power into it from my hips. It ricochets off the door. I go, pick it up, try again.

Justice

THIS PUNISHMENT STARTS VERY MUCH LIKE THE LAST. I'll never stand here again, waiting to gut one of my own. This knowledge is the only way I can put one foot in front of the other.

I open my eyes on the last punishment morning and there is no sadness, or guilt; there are no thoughts of home. The feeling around me is urgent, focused, slowed down. We are going into battle once more.

I climb out of the blankets into the cold, putting a hand to the small of my back, trying to get the twinge in my side to back off by pressing my fingers into it. I feel the weight of the walls around me pressing in, too.

I stretch out a little and I find my shoes, and I think

about the women in this building, and the next one and the next, and those in the shanties. These women and I feel the same about what is to happen, more or less. I know this deep in my bones.

I throw a blanket over me and I go quickly downstairs, drawn to the others. As usual the fires are being lit by the elderly, wearing far too little for the chilly air, with bare feet on the cold ground. There's no wind at all, and mist so thick I cannot see the sky but I feel the city all around me as it goes about its business in the usual way.

It's early but there are a few up. I am amongst the first to throw freezing water over my face. The water is so cold that my skin reddens and my fingers swell up, but I go on, throwing water under my armpits, letting the icy droplets run down my ribs, till I'm sure that I'm fully awake.

I go back then into the relative warmth of the building and head towards the dorms: banshees with lowered heads step aside for me in the hallways.

In my troop's dorm, Agata is scratching her newly shorn head and yawning, Aoife is whispering furiously to Lin, Sene is working through her push-ups on the bit of clear space she's bullied out of the others. Some will have their rituals done already: the rubbing of a lucky stone, a certain number of pull-ups on the doorframe. I let myself smile a little; I feel my shoulders come down about two fingers from their hunch up around my neck. The banshees see me and they look up and they smile. Lin throws something at me, someone's balled-up, sweaty old wraps.

We'll be OK, is what I think. I mean, maybe we'll die, but we're OK.

We put our heads together. Together, silently, we hope Agata can fight well with her injury. Hope that Mare can fight at all after what she's going to go through. That we'll kill Boyle and whoever else needs to die today, that we'll clear the plinth. I hope that I will speak well. Maybe we can come out the other side of this. Doing our best to protect.

I touch my one good throwing knife, packed against my ankle, and when I close my eyes I can feel fingers brush against mine. *Use it.*

Walking west again, my fourth time on that road. Towards home.

I wish I'd had time to have more dreams. I wish I'd let myself feel what I'd lost reach out to me. I wish I'd let myself grieve more. Nobody will remember Maeve and my mother if I die today, nobody will have the dreams of them I do. What a loss that would be to this world.

When we leave the room there'll be an end to the levity, so we linger, saying nearly nothing to each other but being in the same small place, together, safe for now. I sit with the others and we watch Sene doing what she needs to, the smooth mesmerising working of her arms and her back muscles. She is sweating even in the cold. She will do anything to not think of Mare this morning.

We know already that when a punishment bears no relation to a crime, and where crimes against us are not met with rebuke, the justice system can only be a measure of control. This control is not flexed against the immediate victims of these punishments, but against us all. Punishments are a punishment, and a warning and a tactic.

A punishment is an opportunity too. We will make it so.

In the square to the front of our building we gear up as best we can, with the special good clothes they – we – wear for missions: glad rags we stash away, secret riches, for use when it really matters. The banshees are getting ready their mouth-coverings, they are putting on their best forearm guards, reinforced with worn rubber cut from the wheels of long-rusted cars on the road. I see long-secreted shoes on the feet of banshees I know well; I see wire twisted around fingers to make those punches felt. Ears are covered with lengths of fabric to help protect them. Hair is greased and charcoal from the fire is drawn across the multitude of colours and shades and textures of skin. We share our scant riches, we check and admire each other, a ceremony of love and bonding as well as preparation.

Here's what I put on me now:

My hair I slick back with grease and I secure with a thin strip of fabric tied tight around my head, hiding my one ruined ear and helping keep my good one from sticking out and looking tempting. My cheeks are daubed with charcoal to draw off the sun from my eyes, should it ever come out. I wear my best vest and over it my best shirt; some fabric that cleaves to my skin and keeps me warm but mobile. Over it I've my arm guards, built from rubber and tied with wire, which I use on one finger of each hand too. I throw out a couple of punches into the cold air.

I've been saving the black stretching trousers; they've good manoeuvrability but they're light so I wrap black fabric around where I can to reinforce, and I stretch out and make sure they're not getting in the way of themselves. My shoes are good, worn in carefully, trustworthy.

My knives, my knives, my knives. Adorning the wall of some man who does not know the pointed end from the handle. There are a lot of questions those knives could have answered today.

Management will not know the subtle languages of

our clothes. This is not ordinary punishment-day wear, but they will not be able to read us.

We go out and limber up after we dress. We banish the cold from our muscles, pushing up from our knuckles in the dirt till we can feel the hot rich blood pulsing into our toes and fingers and the tips of our noses, Sene with the rest of us though she's warmed up plenty already. We work our fingers till they can pluck an imaginary knife from a belt and throw it smooth and clean and quick.

I keep an eye on Agata beside me, her powerful form swathed in mist. She straps on a breastplate she's made – or her girlfriend has – from boring small holes in a thin metal sheet and strapping it over her shoulders, and when she's ready I go to help her, fixing the loop on the back, checking her guards. I stand while she does the same, patting from my shoulders along my arms and all the way down. When she stands again, nodding that I'm dressed well, we let our eyes meet. We rest our foreheads together, her breath in mine, listening to the other banshees around us, doing the things they do before they go into battle. Here is how we communicate, being kept from education, being kept silent. I try to feel that Agata and I are two arms of the one body again. We'll need that back to fight well.

We are ready: the thick and thin of us, the tall and the

short, the loud and quiet, the dark and the light, all of us angry, all of us quick, all of us just *done*. Past done we had to get, all of us. All of us with love for each other through the things we do together.

We finish our checks and we get up together, and together we begin to move. Around us, Ash's other troops get ready, B-Troop just behind us, greenuns watching in awe. As first troop, A-Troop, we're to go first, and they part to let us pass, nodding, checking our equips in admiration, open mouthed at us, some of them.

We go through the city, two by two, Agata and me leading the troop, Aoife and Lin following close. Behind us, holding so much furious energy that she's frightening even to look at, comes Sene. We're solid, we're a unit. We're unstoppable.

The mist is lifting up off us and the sun's dirty fingers reach out through the clouds down to us, as if to try and help lift us up out of this horror. We can only do this ourselves.

We are moving.

We jog in formation down towards the zoo. Somewhere in the gaols I know that Mare will be awake. With the end in sight. What a thing to do for us; what a thing to step forwards, to offer up her own flesh and blood.

And in the other upper parts of the city, management get ready too. They talk together, perhaps, about the damage they will do, and what this young woman deserves. They are frightened, I suppose, beneath it. If they were children you'd correct them. Some of them looking away, something of them looking right at it all and nodding, goading on. Taking pleasure. I hate them with an easy fury and I hold this fury close to me, shape it and watch it grow.

I think of Mare. Look at what this woman will give for the rest of us. The selfless act demands we look to ourselves and ask what we would give; what violence would we do upon ourselves or let be done. What painful judgement would we call down upon ourselves to show up the terrible system once more. How many women have been willing to give up their own selves for the good of others, generation after generation? Today, things will change.

The mist begins to lift and Phoenix City allows itself slowly to be seen: the good buildings to our back now, the parts of farmland with the young men and old. The good men, strong and hard-working, who'd fight with us, Aoife says, and those who'll try to fight us. We shall see soon enough.

We're warming now and I can feel that good healthy sweat amongst us, that scent of supple strong bodies opening up to the day. It's hard not to feel as if we're headed out on a mission; it's hard not to feel hopeful.

The road curves a little to the right beneath our feet and we're facing nearly directly into the rising sun now. We are joined by nobody as we walk; where banshees go there's nothing that'll get in the way. But we keep watch all around, and when we pass those on the road I see a group of young men coming from the farmers' barracks, nodding with steely, ready faces. I see clusters of breeders standing aside to let us pass, the youngest holding their fresh faces against the morning light, the older and the wealthier shrouded in fabric, but all with their eyes on us. It is morning and it is quiet but the city is alive. Where there are people, there is hope.

Or women, anyway.

At the zoo I direct the troop to help finish gathering men and women. We must gather the children as well. They start their learning young here, so they do – management will have this thing taught – and today can be no different from usual. As I watch, more people from the shanties are brought out by the hair, pulled by the sure angry fists of banshees I do not know well, and by some I do.

It takes a long time for near three thousand souls – the working wallers are the only ones to be let off – to get organised along the road the way they should to partake as individuals in this, our one communal activity.

We move tall and straight, and we try to look like the

law. Around us, more bodies press in to the sides of the road, and that feeling I get of being crushed with them, as if there is not enough air in the world and not enough sky and I will sink under a great weight. I close my eyes and breathe in deep, trying to breathe past somehow the smell of old sweat and bad food and sourness. I breathe out.

I feel cool fingers reach for my hand, and when I open my eyes Agata gives me a half-look to let me know she sees me and she knows. She takes my hand gently and I let myself entwine my fingers with hers, to move my body a little closer, maybe for the last time. I close my eyes again.

We make our way to our place at the Broken Finger.

Even with the quiet of the city I can hear feet moving against earth and cracked concrete, bodies moving through the undergrowth that has found its way up everywhere it's given a chance, brushing against skin, fabric against fabric, sighs, coughs, snuffles and sneezes.

People are animals first.

While my banshees push and shove to make breathing space around me, I keep my eyes closed. I allow myself off to stand on a beach.

I go to Slanbeg for a last time. I think of my house, the quiet rooms, the dusty books, the floorboards that have creaked under our weights, the handles worn thin through the use of our hands. The house empty because my mothers have gone to the beach to hold hands on the sand and look across the waves. I let myself walk towards them. The air is fresh and clean. I do not go so far as to imagine a gentle hand brushing my hair.

I open my eyes again, suddenly, sickeningly present.

The punishment has begun.

We have all done this thing to her; for us she allows this thing to be done.

I breathe deep and I try to keep my mind blank, but my thoughts cannot keep from Mare's body, tall and dark, and what she will go through now, is going through now, this moment. The fear she must be feeling, her beautiful smooth skin to be pierced again and again, torn violently with blunt objects, hurt, and for what? The pitilessness of it. Those who can still feel for another, we feel it. I have to believe we do. I have to believe there are enough of us to change the world.

Where we are we cannot see her coming yet. She will be making her way along the road, with two banshees behind her and two in front, banshees she doesn't know in case she's let have one moment of hope or comfort on this, her long walk. But she knows us. She'll see me at the end.

It takes time. I always forget how *long* it all goes on. I finger where my knives should be and squint my eyes against the sun. Nobody is giving anything away and I can only wonder who'll be with us.

There's shuffling along the line and at last she is coming this way. Bringing my eyes away from the horizon of wall against sky, and towards the place where she is stepping forwards is one of the worst little things I have ever had to do; raising my eyes, so heavy, to witness her pain, taken on for all of us, and letting this moment bleed into the next and the next.

I can see the top of her head, short grey hair and the pain of that is fresh, her delicate fingers so recently and carefully making herself presentable for this display. The head bobbles just out of sight, leaning more one way than the other – a limp.

The worst is over, I think, feeling a sudden surge of new hope. The worst is over and she's still standing.

A little behind me, Lin whistles low through her teeth to say, 'She's bad,' and, ahead of us, Aoife glances over her shoulder to us. She's tears in her eyes and she's blinking a lot to keep them at bay. No crying for banshees, especially somewhere public. It is not done; we are not to have feelings.

Here she comes; and now here he comes, the great bald pate drawing all eyes on it as it makes its way towards us. Boyle's people are looking for me to go to him, and I hang back just another minute, keeping my eyes on Mare – I just get a glimpse of her face, sweating, pale beneath its darkness, bloodied, her eyes lowered to the ground, long eyelashes thrown down over her cheeks – but my arm is pulled and it is time to go and do my own duty for the city.

The men come, and when they put their hands on me I can't shrink from them. They dig their hands into the flesh of my shoulders, and my feet are already moving where they want me to go. Any little opportunity for control or coercion, they will take it and take and take and take. I lift my chin and, for now, I let their hands do what they please, in front of everyone, same as anywhere else.

I walk to where the great bald pate stands at the top of the steps, on the wide part of the finger pointing out over the wall. I climb up the few steps to join him. I can feel the angry energy, I can feel his hairless bulk getting ready to speak. There's boiling satisfaction and something nearly like arousal coming off him. He raises his great meaty hands and whatever little noise this silent city was making quiets further. His soft, colourful garments, finished with a great scarf worn by so many management, ruffle a little against the breeze. I look up to see again children in their rags, the weak with nothing to stave off the last shivers of the morning.

As I look out I catch sight of Mare. She has fallen to her knees, but the eyes of the crowd are drawn to this man who is making as if to speak, and nobody has noticed but the banshees around her. Discreetly they help her up; she makes it along another few paces, is spared however many people in those few steps would have done her harm, according to their duties as have been prescribed by this city.

She moves along, bent over double, blood pouring from the wounds on her arms, her chest, stomach, her thighs and breast. I cannot see her beautiful face.

The worst is over, I think. I have to think the worst is over. It must get better from here. If it gets worse than this there will be no living.

There are other things to see, from my vantage point: some wallers stand, with their tools in their hands always, near the foot of the wall to my right, the south.

There are injured men to the fore of the crowds, men such as I've seen more and more of around the city, working slowly forwards with sticks under each arm, the more important or popular being supported by others. Pale-faced, shaken, even under their swathes of expensive fabrics. Management all.

Boyle begins to speak, his voice booming, spit flecking from him through the air, teeth obscenely white and rich inside his fat healthy mouth. He has rings on his fingers, smooth round ones, not like the spiky, uncomfortable, dangerous ones we've to wear.

'Citizens!'

I swear I can feel in my bones the army of the undead outside the city gates come together to freeze, to take in for a moment the heartening noise of a man's voice, to still and turn their heads towards his voice, towards the heat of all of us, to allow their proboscises to lean towards to us, swelling, dripping, hungry. All of this was such a terrible idea. Every single decision a bad one and a mean one. Still he speaks on.

'We are gathered today to do justice to this woman.'

He allows the hush to fall again; I can feel the skrake outside the walls scrabble for us against the borders of the city. I can feel their dead fingers on the walls as if they were scratching against my own skin. Strange to think that management cannot feel this; they have no empathy or feeling or insight for the city they rule. They cannot feel that it is ready to crumble around them.

Mare has fallen again to her knees, just a few feet away from us now. I try not to look at her; I cannot keep my eyes off her. Between words I can hear her blood drop heavily to the hard-packed earth, her life ebb away while we watch.

'These betrayals happen too often,' Boyle shouts, and we all agree in our own ways. 'Let this teach the traitors amongst you; we will not accept dissent.'

He gestures for me, again without looking at me – the

way he might not glance at a hammer in his hand. The distance between the person he is and the person I am is insurmountable; the difference between our lives and our futures renders any real exchange impossible, unthinkable.

'Make her stand,' he says quietly to the men and women around him, nodding to Mare, and they move towards her, lifting her under her arms. Her feet scrabble for purchase but they seem too weak to hold her up.

There are hands on me again, urging me forwards, and then his palm and fingers are on my back.

'Good girl,' he says.

I take a breath, open my mouth. I cannot allow myself to think now or I will let it all pass. If I lose this moment, we lose everything.

I let the quiet hang for an instant. I wait till I know they're listening.

'I cannot stay silent,' I shout, 'about the things we all know happen in this city.'

Beside me Boyle nods one long nod and then rests his chin on his chest, his eyes closed.

I pause to let the silence stretch and protract. I stand on a precipice again; behind me is the past and in front is only emptiness, waiting to be filled, but I can stop, here, for a moment and look about me. Three thousand pairs of eyes look towards me, dirty faces lifted upwards to watch me and see duty carried out, to see the justice of their city done.

Today they will get it.

'Today!' I shout. 'Today, everything changes!'

I let the bald man stir himself and step forwards, and together we go to the plinth and stand on it, he first and me alone now helping Mare. He holds in his hand the knife for the last part of the spectacle.

'See, Orpen, Outlier! The one who ran so far for the honour of calling this city home,' he says. 'Truly there is no alternative; to attempt to leave is to endanger us all. To leave is to betray! Betrayal of the city is betrayal of the self.'

The three of us stay another moment on the big square podium – he and I standing tall, looking about us, Mare slumped and breathing heavily, her blood running off her into the stone of the monument.

Boyle nods, and brandishes the knife again. Together Mare and I turn to walk the broken path out to the wall, with himself behind us, holding the handle of the knife almost idly. He's already thinking about the next thing: going back to his buildings, drinking his good clean water, his fucking dinner. It shows, it always shows.

Mare's steps are slow and so painful; still I cannot get a good look at her face. We go some way before I risk breathing.

'Any small thing I can do?'

She does not reply.

'Mare,' I whisper, trying to infuse all my found love and tenderness for her into that word.

I breathe deep and try to move her along without looking like I'm helping much. Her body feels heavy underneath my arm; I'm working hard. The monument is just two hundred steps or so long, up a gentle incline to where the tip of the finger breaks the wall. The distance goes slow and quick all at once. The skrake closer with each step, reaching, shrieking.

Here we are, alive, putting one foot in front of the other. We're still moving, so we are.

I can feel his meaty breath down the back of my neck but we walk on and I do not turn around. The eyes of all are upon us, whether in pity or expectation, waiting for the next thing to happen. I am glad for our warm-up stretches this morning. Discreetly I roll my shoulders, take some deep breathe through the nose; I try to meet myself where I am.

We are at the end of the plinth now. Now is the time. We stop.

'The worst is over,' I say beneath my breath.

'It's just beginning,' Mare says, her voice stronger than I'd have thought possible.

We turn till we are facing him, or I am at least. Mare

is still stooped over, her eyes squeezed shut against the pain. There's a big shard of plastic sticking out of her arm and I want to grab it and pull it out, but the bleeding is bad already and I don't want to be making decisions like that for her.

We stand, the wind of the day beginning to rise.

Before us, he brandishes his knife again, holds it up to catch the light, to catch the eyes of the hordes around us in case they miss anything. I am so glad he has no training; I'm so glad to know he won't stab Mare with one smooth easy movement from there. I have plenty of time.

He moves quicker than I'd have thought, though. It's his impatience to get on with things, to count this job as done, and duty served. The knife comes down towards Mare but as it comes I reach for mine, hidden well under the tunic, the knife given me by the last banshee that stood on this plinth waiting to be thrown to the skrake horde reaching for us again now.

I stab him in the stomach.

I haven't the grip on the handle that I'd have liked and the blade isn't long, but in the stop-start time, those few life-changing moments we all experience, I know that the movement is good. The knife goes in as far as the hilt and my hand comes awkwardly against the layers of fabric he has on him. I pushed hard and deep and now I wonder was it enough, and I try to move it, to cause all the damage I can. His own hand does not let go of his blade but he stops mid-air.

Shocked, he is so *shocked*, he cannot fathom what is happening up here on this violent plinth in front of all the people he works day and night to terrorise. All he can do is look down, blinking, at his own self and see the handle of the knife stuck in him. I watch his expression change from one of open blankness to pure fury. He wields his knife again, his face screwing up now to red horror, to go for me.

I try to pull my blade free but my fingers are slippery with sweat and the knife does not come. Boyle has his paw-like hands raised, his small eyes wide as they'll go with apoplectic anger, and those big hands shove my chest so hard the breath goes out of me.

This man must be two or nearly three times my weight.

I am thrown towards the very end of the pointed plinth, landing hard on my back.

The knife, still in him.

A lot is happening very, very quickly now. All I can do is blink, and it's just as well that for a moment I lie still. My head and back rest on the tapered end of the plinth, right the way over the wall. If I lose my balance now, or try to work too fast, I'll fall into the mass of skrake beneath me.

I do not move, but every breath I take here is a moment

I'll be badly missed where I'm needed. Before me, just a few paces further up on the plinth I see Mare, still bent double, blood dripping steadily from her wounds, her face . . .

I breathe out a quick huff, raise my legs high in the air and use them to propel my body upright. I flip up, landing solid, ready to go.

Ahead of me the scene is laid out simply. Four paces from me the bulk of our leader looms over the small, cowering figure of Mare. Behind them, where the base of the finger reaches its broken knuckle, there is movement: men, management, moving awkwardly because of the thick clothes they have wrapped around them, but as quick as they can, to aid their leader.

But.

There's nowhere to go but forwards.

Neither Boyle nor I will die alone.

With all my small might I throw myself into the air, spin, and catch Boyle in the chest with my full weight, getting right on to the hilt of the knife sticking out of him, which must hurt. He staggers backwards, and as I land I jump again and sink a flying punch into his throat. He staggers again, his legs weakening beneath him. I stretch forwards with him, grasp the handle of the knife and this time, grip tight as I pull it out.

A knife in my hand again.

The four men running for their leader have covered half the distance between us already; the leader is already getting up, heavy and slow but nothing wrong with him except surprise and lack of training.

And the kinfe in his gut.

I look over my shoulder to Mare, a great gust throwing the wind towards her. I hold out my hand.

She takes it, the strength of her grip strengthening me.

She gets to her feet, taller than me, stronger, the better banshee in every way.

Her head is the last thing to rise up, and when it does I see how clear it is of pain and fear.

She is ready, furious, pure warrior.

She takes a small moment to pull out the worst shards of plastic lodged into her skin. She lets the blood flow; she looks at me and the corners of her mouth pull back just a twitch, and in that instant I'd die for her a thousand times.

I toss her the knife I just pulled out of the leader and reach for the one hidden in my back armour; I pull it down and brandish it as Mare grips hers.

We stand together.

We move forwards.

In a battle, sense suggests that you take down whoever can do most damage first. In hand-to-hand combat, when the skills of any one opponent is unknown, that decision will be dictated by weight alone.

Boyle is a big man. We go through him like sharp blades, treating him like any other monster we'd meet on the road. His face is gone blank again; he cannot understand what is happening. He would not have been able, even without the wound in his belly and his windpipe bruised. He never had cause to develop the language for what we are and what we can do.

He stands on both feet unsteadily, blinking at us, hands raised now in defence.

I feint a jab to his nose and he flinches back; Mare, with her better reach, makes a good clean slice to his neck.

We could leave him staggering where he is or we could do worse. We have maybe five breaths before the first of those other men reach us. We make it count.

He reaches for Mare and I swerve under his arm and throw my shoulder into the small of his back. He stumbles forwards, more than he meant to, one hand to his throat to try and stanch the flow of blood. Mare grabs the hand that was reaching for her and pulls hard before ducking under it and together we shove forwards and forwards, not letting him stop.

We let his momentum carry him forwards over the end of the plinth.

We watch him fall to the ravenous shriekers below us.

I *think* I hear him scream, but we are already turning to face the next one who comes, getting a few steps forwards away from the dangerous end of the monument.

The first man coming now is small, and running too fast, uncontrolledly; his face, so different from the leader's, is screwed up and red with rage in just the same way. If we got out of his way I think he'd run straight to the edge of the plinth and jump off after him. We should maybe let him, but I can't help throwing out an arm across his neck to give him pause. He goes down harder than either one of us suspected, landing with a thump on his back, and I jump on to him, pinning his arms down with my knees. I go to work with my knife, letting him have its mercy quick as I can.

These soft men are much easier to go through than the monsters we're better used to. Did they not guess that we'd come for them, eventually? Some are tall, some thin despite their good food, but they all crumple the same.

I'm aware of the shape of Mare moving past me and meeting the next of the men. I make sure the one beneath me will not get up again and then I rise to join her.

Side by side we walk the length of the plinth back the way we came.

The second one comes on, bigger than both of us again, but with two of us who know what we're doing, he's no bother. He makes for Mare first, horrified that she, though punished and bleeding, is far from dead.

Mare ducks him and while he's extended I drive my shin hard into the back of his knee and he drops, surprised. They're always surprised, and you've a moment then to make it count. His thigh is handy then to step up and get my own leg round his neck. I swing my body weight around till he's knocked off balance. He goes down, and Mare is on him with her knife.

The third comes for me, making his choice because I'm smaller, or I'm a step ahead, or he has his eye on me anyway, and he throws himself into me. He's not huge but his weight is plenty enough to slam me back down. I tighten my stomach muscles, make sure to keep the back of my head from busting against the crumbling old concrete, breathe out so I'm not winded again, and almost before his full weight comes to rest upon mine it eases up again. Mare pulls him by the hair till his head is wrenched up and he's made to reckon with her: I knee him in the groin, which is a move I've had a hankering to try on someone who'll really feel it. Works nicely, so it does.

It's easy to shove him over the side of the monument. He crashes hard into the packed dirt and I get a glimpse of him being surrounded by a mob of the city, but I cannot watch – will they help him up and come for us too, raging? – as we've the last of those first four men to contend with. This one has stopped a good ten paces from us and he is standing stock-still, looking not at us but over the side of the plinth towards the place we threw the third man. At ten paces his face is white, his eyes wide. He looks like he's going to throw up. Instead he backs off a few paces, turns, runs.

It's hard not to laugh.

We've the plinth to ourselves now, Mare and me, standing tall, high up where the air feels nearly fresh. The sky above us clean and spare, the clouds moving with the wind, blowing west. I could be on the road again tonight, I think.

I look to Mare, who is watching the crowd around us. She is bleeding still but standing so tall. She catches my eye and she smiles.

For almost the first time I think, *I could go home.*

There is shouting coming from the bottom of the plinth – management and their supporters trying to get to Mare and me, pushing and shoving – but for now, for a moment, we're safe, and the rest of the crowd is still absolutely silent.

'I came here six years ago,' I tell them. 'Every day since that day I've been made to do things I don't want to do. I've been told by management to beat and to wreck.'

I shake my head at them, speaking slowly. 'I don't

want to do it any more. I want to tell you I'm sorry. Me and my troop all are.'

I think of how proud Mam and Maeve would be if they could see me in this moment, and that thought makes my eyes fill with tears. This is why, I realise. So I could imagine two long-dead women loving me anew.

'I can take you to where I came from, an island to the west. It's safe, there are no skrake there. It's three days' walk; it will be dangerous. I can only promise that me and the other banshees who come will try to protect you.'

I try to get a read from the crowd but I can only see blank, shocked faces.

'You've no reason to trust me,' I say. 'But this city is going to stay the same or get worse. If you think you deserve better, if you want to try to live freer, come with us.'

I take a breath, focus. Nearly there.

'We meet at the zoo gates. Gather whatever you need and can carry, bring water and food if you have them. We leave now.'

'The skrake will get us!'

A deep voice, not too far from the front, shouts at me. He doesn't sound frightened as he shouts, but he's not wrong.

'It's true, there are skrake. They might attack us on

the road. But they might break down the walls, you might get sick here, or on the island. We cannot choose how we die in this world. But there is choice in how we live.'

I didn't hope for cheers. I try once more.

'This silence won't save you. Come with us if you want to live!'

The end of my little speech is met with absolute quiet. I look about me, deflated, self-conscious, and Mare catches my eye. She tilts her chin left to let me know to look north. I can see a big group at the back of the crowd making its way off – the groups are just shapes from here, but there might be hundreds of them, moving back north together, up the road. I look east and see others going towards the zoo. There are so many, peeling off in all directions. The crowd is thinning, and closer to the platform, beneath us, there is murmuring and then shoving.

But with one thing over and the next just beginning, we have this moment, before the next battle, to reach down our arms to lift up the other women. Sene is first, tears in her eyes, checking over Mare, who loosens some of the material around her throat and body. Her cuts are bad, one in her arm especially, which bleeds freely. Sene throws her arms around her, holds her close a moment, and brings her a little way off down the finger so she can

236

sit her down and tend to her. She'll be safer there than anywhere, with all of us between herself and the people who want to kill her. Sene has a little bottle and, as I watch, Mare takes it and drinks thirstily.

I don't have the shakes and sweats yet and that's how I know the battle isn't over. Where are the wallers, where the other banshees? Where's the next fight coming from?

The rest of the team is on us, Agata launching herself and throwing her arms around me, telling me in my good ear that she loves me before streaking off down the steps and away again into the crowd. I'm laughing still, too relieved to try to stop or go after her. Aoife is shrieking and whooping, Lin grimly determined, but both keeping watch like we are on a mission all the same, which I appreciate.

I shake my head and try to remember to celebrate this little win. It always seems obvious afterwards which way actions were going to play out, but we thought – we discussed – what would happen if the city mobbed us up here, if there were so many who disagreed with us that they'd attack us right away for throwing some of management to the skrake. There were a few, but the banshees didn't let them through. They will have gone off to regroup, I suppose. But we have the now.

Banshees are still clambering up to the podium, grabbing and hugging me. My troop reaches down to the long-haired women too, pulling them up, and I think, this is good. It has to be all of us up here, everyone who wants. I keep a handy eye around us, knowing that all the same we'll need to move soon. Our little band is an easy target up here.

If the city was a person it would be just about to make its mind up about something, and decisions can be violent occasions. To the south, I'm surprised to see fire-smoke already, blackness billowing up into the clearing skies.

Where is Agata?

Getting Out

'WE'VE GOT TO GO,' SENE IS SHOUTING AT ME FROM her position by Mare. 'We have to move quick, before they can get organised.'

I have time to be amazed that she's looking to me to give the orders. She's right, we've spent too long up here already. We have to get to the gates. I shield my eyes against the sun and look past the already dispersing crowds, half expecting to see B-Troop leading a mass towards us, knives raised. Instead, all I see is smoke, black and billowing, from the east, the old city gates.

A soft whupping noise by my ear and I turn back to Sene.

Her eyes have flown open wide in shock and she puts

a hand to her temple before the second stone hits her, hard, right in her throat, and a third. She puts her arms around her head to protect herself.

I step towards her, get my body in front of hers, shielding her and Mare as best I can. A hail of stones hits my back while I wait for the rest of the troop to see, and to do what they need to do.

The first part of the plan is done, and we've had all the celebrating we are likely to get. More than we deserve, probably.

'To the gates!' I shout, pitching my voice high so that it'll be heard above the din.

Even before I've finished yelling, more stones come, one hitting hard in the back of my head, making my eyes sting and bringing a taste of copper to the back of my throat. Hands reach for us and it's a risk to look down now, but I have to, blinking hard, feeling confused and suddenly overwhelmed.

'Who is throwing?' I ask, helping them get Mare gently down the last few steps.

'A small group, mostly management,' says a woman with long white hair.

'Some stayed to see what damage they could do.'

I look up the plinth to see if my troop are being hit. They're standing straight, eyes out to the crowd, fearless.

'They've stopped,' I say, and I turn a little gingerly to face the direction the firing was coming from.

'They were stopped,' the woman says.

'Banshees?' Sene asks, blinking against the light.

'No! Just . . . people.'

A group of men is making its way up the steps, the men moving surely, with purpose, and I get ready to take them on, standing again as shield to Mare, Sene squaring up beside me. Four of them, one with a long straight stick. Huge.

As I watch he takes the last few steps at a run and just as I get up to face him, my heart sinking, not knowing in that instant if Agata is there to fight with me and knowing that without her I'll lose this, the man turns, brandishes his stick. Protecting us. His friends – men and women, I'm seeing now – catch up and do the same.

Aoife and Lin are only a few steps behind me, Agata and Sene helping Mare down from the platform. She is taking the steps carefully. The blood isn't pouring off her, but she's pale, shivering even in the warmth of the day.

Together we head not that long way back to the barracks but to the zoo – closer, and prepared for us, all being well.

Now that we're moving, I can think a moment and take stock of my injuries: a stinging headache, that knot again growing in the back of my head like a fist. The usual pain in my side, below the ribs and back a little. And still, and still. I feel jubilant.

Jubilant is not the right feeling to have.

'Hold on,' I tell Mare. 'Just hold on.'

I will not look too closely at her, not till we can do something about her injuries, but I keep a keen eye on those around us: the men who helped, Sene more than half-carrying Mare from her opposite side, Aoife and Lin, some long-haired women like a shield around us.

We could talk, now, like outside, if we wanted; if we had things to say to each other. That feeling of jubilation bubbles up again and I squash it down. Not yet.

Agata is feeling even more present with her absence. I know where she is, I suppose.

The gates to the zoo are not far from the Broken Finger and already we can make them out. Already people are gathering. Perhaps two dozen. We'll have to give the city time, time to gather what they need, their loved ones and to come to us, though in doing so we allow the enemy to gather too.

To our right as we jog, off towards the massive old city doors, the smoke is black and thick.

It's no accident, I realise grimly, whatever is going on down there. At least one of us will have to see what is happening.

The gates at last. The people standing there, packs strapped to them or, if they've no cloth for packs, items held in bare hands: shovels, spikes, papers, bundles. They stare at us silently, at Sene especially, and part to let us through.

Aoife leads on through the labyrinth of corrugated iron and sheet metal walls. We have not come far from the zoo gates when she ducks into a dwelling to check it, comes out to shake her head and lead us to another. A nod.

Inside, is a neat dark space with a low cot to one side, a place Mare can rest. Lin produces a canteen from her robes and presses it to her lips. Mare is breathing heavily and shivering. Sene sits gently beside her, reaches for her hand.

'Doesn't hurt,' she says, through gritted teeth.

'I know it,' Sene says quietly. 'It'll get better.'

These injuries will take a long time to heal, I know, and every break of the skin is an invitation to go wrong, to get red and swollen and itchy, to invite the sweats; to kill. We've all seen it. The chances of anyone healing from these wounds, a hundred cuts, at least one serious stab wound – the chances are small. But Mare is not anyone.

At the door, Lin gestures me towards her.

'Close your eyes,' I tell Mare. 'You've not long to rest. We're getting out of the city soon.'

A few steps from the hut I speak quietly to Lin and Aoife.

'She's not going to make it,' says Lin.

'She might,' I say. 'She'll have a chance, at least.'

'Where's Agata?'

I smile. 'You know Agata.'

'We do,' Lin nods. 'Hard for you. Not much of a partner.'

I meet her eyes, surprised. 'Better than I deserve.'

'Where do you want us?'

'Let Mare rest a small while,' I tell them. 'Once she can move, let her and Sene lead through the first group. Children and elderly, but a few fighters, too, if you can. We'll be lucky not to attract any attention from the skrake.'

'And then?'

'Stay at the gates, keep guiding people through, a steady stream. Hopefully more banshees will join. Let some of them through to guard the people, but keep more back. Just in case.'

'What will you do?' Aoife asks.

'The fire,' I say. 'That's no coincidence.'

Lin nods once, sharp, and Aoife touches my arm. 'Should we go with you?'

I shake my head. Better on my own.

'Go,' I tell them, and as they turn to leave I remember.

'Find those men who helped at the monument. They'll help again if they're let.'

'We'll see you at the gates.'

They go back inside the dwelling and I turn and run in the direction of the smoke, weaving my way through the shanties again towards the zoo gates. There are more people there now, and I'm moving too quickly for them to notice me and make way.

On the other side, headed towards the old city doors, I pause at a small rise and look back. There are too many to count quickly, but tens of people, perhaps as many as a hundred.

The smell of burning intensifies as I near the old doors. I remember everything I can about them: our daily runs over the little catwalks at the top of them. Had they been shored up with earth by the wallers? I thought so: but they were made of wood, wood dried and crisped in the heat of the sun. I grit my teeth.

As I run I think of the things I'm afraid of. Not seeing Agata again. Meeting B-Troop. Meeting just about anyone, come to think of it. I'm fair game to anyone now as a traitor. I slow and unravel one of my hand wraps, working the sweaty material around my nose and mouth. A poor disguise but it might give people pause and it helps a little with the smoke.

The smoke is so black it's hard to get close.

A figure, ahead of me, shrouded in black. I can tell by the way she moves who it is and I nearly turn away before a huge crack breaks through even the noise of the fire and I see that a part of the great door is ready to give way. If I squint hard enough I'm sure I'll see the necrotic reaching arms of the skrake pushing through the cracked wood to get in, burning what's left of their flesh to the dead bone.

I watch the figure of Ash beating back the flames. If I try to help her, she'll almost certainly kill me.

If I don't, the skrake will get through.

I turn, thinking if I run back to the gates I'll find someone else to help her keep the horde from the city, and jump out of my skin shouting a regrettable little cry – I can see her.

'Agata!'

The pure relief.

'I looked for you at the gates!'

'The fire,' I shout back. 'The skrake will get through!'

She nods, her calm eyes looking over the scene while she thinks.

There's a happy look to her. The flames reflected in her eyes.

And then, she's gone from me. Flying straight towards Ash, her hands stretched out either side of her, blades of some description in either.

I run with her, hardly knowing what I'm doing.

Ash's back is turned to us as she beats back flames with a length of something.

The heat.

There's a heroism in Ash beating back the flames, focused totally on her task.

Agata goes for her.

I lunge and get nearly between them somehow, my shout giving Ash time enough to turn, to see Agata's blades in her hands.

'Agata!' I shout, showing her my palm.

'It's the perfect opportunity!' Agata shouts. 'Don't you see? She'll kill us, if she can!'

I hesitate. She's right.

She senses it, knows every bend of my thought, and she reaches out again.

Ash squares up to her, coming to her full height.

I stand between them, hands out to either, unsure what I'm going to do.

Ash, the best fighter of us, the heaviest, with the greatest reach, but unarmed as far as I can see.

Agata, with her fury and blades.

Whatever time I have to think is gone.

'Orpen,' Ash says. 'Fight with me!'

She thinks I'm the deciding factor here, I realise.

'Stay!' she says urgently. 'We can build something

good here.' Ash looks so deeply into my eyes, even in all the chaos, I feel off balance. 'Nobody else needs to die, Orpen. We can stop this.'

She's offering me pardon. Pardon and partnership.

'Can't you come with us?' I ask, only realising when I speak that I'm crying.

Ash glances at Agata, who is watching us silently. She shakes her head.

And Agata chooses this moment to fly at her.

Ash moves so eloquently, as if she knew just how Agata would come for her. She trained her, after all. She uses the sacking she's been fighting the fire with to wrap around one of Agata's blades, she pulls and I think Agata lets go, moving instead to get to her with her left hand. Ash guards herself with her knee and rebounds a little, still caught by her other arm, which lets her bring up a licking little kick, right into Agata's face.

Anyone else wouldn't have the power in that leg after a block, but I can feel Agata crumple a little. I know what's going to happen next. Ash will bring down that leg again, pivot off the ground to get her full strength behind it and—

I get in the way of it without thinking, scissoring my right leg into hers.

Trying to keep her back is nearly impossible. The leg still comes up, but Agata has got free and she still has one blade. Quick as Ash, she brings it to her neck. I only realise I have got my arm in the way when I feel the heat and urgency of Agata's skin against mine.

Our eyes meet. Hers are pure determination.

I let go my arm, feeling stung.

I don't believe Ash; I don't believe she can change things because she hasn't changed things. But Ash believes Ash and I know, to her, we are silly, ungrateful girls.

Agata needs my help to beat her and for a moment I hold both of their needs within myself; for a moment I'm a whole future to each of them. I look to Agata and sink my blade deep and quick into Ash's neck, and pull it out again. I try to make it so fast she'll hardly feel it, but already her blood is gurgling up through her mouth.

I hold her hand while the blood runs out of her, I whisper meaningless things to her. It will be OK, I say. I lie down and hold her tight. We'll set things right. You did well, you did the best you could. I tell her all the things I've wanted to tell the dying women around me these last years.

The smoke is all around us, the flames licking up everything dry they can reach.

It does not take long, and when I'm sure she's gone I stand.

Agata's at the gates, sweating and sooty, still holding

the sack Ash had in one hand. I watch, dazed, my vision blurry, trying to make sense of what she's doing.

But she's not trying to put out the fire, she's trying to fan it. She runs to and fro, finding whatever she can to put up against the wood of the gates, to keep the blaze going, pausing to use the sack to get the flames to go higher.

'The doors will burn, the skrake will get through!' I shout. I know she knows this.

'Good!' Agata shouts back over her shoulder. 'Help me!'

I know then that Agata set the fire.

I turn to go back and find the rest of the troop.

The Gates

I MOVE IN A DAZE BACK TOWARDS THE GATES OF THE zoo, Ash's blood drenching my front.

Too much noise in my head to think; the noise of the fire, a screaming coming from far off, getting closer. Agata making the fire, trying to get those old doors to burn. She wants to let the skrake in, I keep thinking, trying to make it make sense. If she wants it, she'll make that happen, one way or another.

Whatever time we have here, it's running out.

The roar in my head becomes even louder till I realise that it's the mass of people I'm seeing, people gathered together who are not afraid of making a racket.

So many at the gates now.

I stumble through them, shouldering people out of the way, and I see then there's a line, making slow progress towards the north. They're being let through slowly to the tunnel.

People are getting out.

Distracted from my own confusion, I run towards Sene's shanty, tripping over a wire and getting up, being turned around before I realise again where I am. The other banshees will be able to set me straight, I know it.

Breathless, I go through the flapped entrance, but the dwelling is empty, the only sign of the others smears of blood left on the cot.

They'll be waiting for me at the gate. In the crowd, I won't have seen them.

I retrace my steps, slower now, breathing carefully.

If they've left, gone through the tunnels, without me . . .

One foot in front of the other, no tripping this time.

Alert.

Some kind of muscle memory working in me, I find myself pausing to pick up a metal bar on the ground, some scrap no longer needed of what I hope is an abandoned dwelling. I feel better with a weapon in my hand.

I'm nearly back at the gates and it's busy, busy as the punishment was. I can see better now, moving amongst the people towards the gate. A line of people moves from the city proper towards the north-east wall, being directed now by people – shanty-dwellers, as far as I can see, along the way. A lot of breeders, their arms around children. I let myself stop and watch, fascinated. It's the younger ones mostly, maybe those more willing to take a risk or hope for a future they haven't seen yet.

Getting through the gates now is difficult. I need to push hard through the steady stream. On the other side I work forwards and then to the right till I'm standing clear again and can look about me. It takes a moment to recognise what it is I'm looking for and then I realise, with something like relief, that I'm looking for the woman with the scar and her child. I want to help them.

From behind, a hand grips my elbow and I turn, the metal bar half raised.

'I told you it was her,' Aoife is saying to Lin. 'Orpen, why are you wearing a mask? We'd never have seen you only for the way you walk around half scalded.'

The fabric around my face, I realise. I unfurl it, the smell of smoke beginning to dissipate a little.

'What happened at the gates?' Lin says, looking at me worriedly.

'Agata,' I say.

'Agata what?' Aoife says. 'Is she OK?'

I nod, thinking of her the way I left her, trying to get

the fire to burn better. Is she still there? Are the skrake close to getting through?

'Mare and Sene?'

'Gone through,' Lin says. 'Mare's not in good shape, Orpen.'

I nod. I can't think about that now.

'Cat?'

'Haven't seen her.'

'She could have gone through without us seeing her. Probably a hundred people are on the other side by now.'

It's hard to imagine them out there. Staying quiet enough not to attract skrake. Moving through the country, headed west. Strange and wonderful. But here at the gates, the weight of responsibility for these people around us is heavy.

'Have you seen . . .' I start, not knowing how to put it. 'Have you seen that woman with the burned face? And her child?'

Blank faces. I give myself a little shake.

'We stay and guard,' I say. 'We help wherever we're needed, wherever there are people being stopped or attacked. Us and the other banshees.'

'Some of the banshees left already,' Lin says, quietly furious.

I can't understand what she means.

'I'd a look around the barracks while I was up there,'

she says. 'A few troops left the usual way, right after the punishment.'

I look away, towards the crowds, while I take this in. My eyes searching for the woman with the scar (if I find her, I'll find her child too), even while my mind works.

'If we told them all, word would've got back to Ash,' Lin says, thinking I'm worrying over the choice we made not to tell all the banshees our plan.

I stay quiet while my eyes rove. I want to hear what Aoife thinks.

'Maybe they'll wait for us,' Aoife says. 'Out there.'

Lin snorts.

'Maybe she's right,' I say. 'They'll need somewhere to go to.'

'Yeah, they might be waiting for us,' Lin says darkly. 'On Ash's orders.'

I hadn't thought of that; a troop of banshees sent ahead maybe, to kill anyone who escapes. My heart thumps at the thought of people getting by the gates, through the tunnel and outside, only to be cut through by the likes of us.

We stand quiet. Ahead of us, people stream up from the northern parts of the city towards the gates, and the gates are full open to let them in.

'Maybe we should go too,' Lin says. 'Won't be long

till whatever resistance there is to this comes at us. No way of knowing how that'll go.'

Aoife is nodding. 'We've done our part,' she says to me, trying to get me to meet her eye. 'More than our part. We can help protect them out there.' Her voice is nearly wheedling, a voice I never heard before from her.

'We're banshees,' I say.

'We know,' Lin says, rolling her eyes.

'When I was growing up I used to see these posters,' I say, 'with pictures of banshees, saying how we were there to protect people, to help people. And then I came here and I saw what banshees actually do. Don't you want to be better than that? Now, *now*, this is the moment we can choose to be better. We can be banshees for real, we just have to be brave enough.'

I'm thinking of my mothers again, and Ash.

There's such a long silence from the others. I can't even bring myself to look at their faces. I wish Agata was with me. It doesn't matter what they do, really, I've to stay. It's just about whether I'll stay alone.

'OK,' Aoife says softly. 'OK, Orpen.'

Lin is quiet.

'C'mon, Lin,' Aoife says.

'You're such fuckers,' she responds after a moment. 'You're going to get us all killed, Outlier.'

I laugh, a quick, brutal noise. She's never been more right.

We move a little closer to the gates, watching now for places we can help, taking up position out front, where we can stand together and watch the people streaming by.

It's nearly soothing to watch.

The people crowd around us, talking, milling together, the breeders with the farmers and the shanties and the wallers. Mixes that you never see. Too few of us in so many ways, but too many, too many to feed or water or keep alive on the road. Lots of children, some of them coming in twos and threes, children leading children.

Three days, I think, *maybe four*. That's all they've to survive. Maybe there'll be help for us then on Slanbeg.

I think of Mare and Sene with them.

Even if there turns out to be nothing else, I have this, this moment of hope. I hold it tight.

'Maybe the noise is no harm,' I say, mostly to myself. 'Keep the skrake focused on the city, maybe we can get out clean.'

Time passes while we watch. I check every face to see has it burn marks. The crowd thins, grows and then thins again. Surely most of whoever has decided to come will have gone through by now. I look for Agata, for Cat, see no sign.

A stir then, a shift of mood that at first I think I'm imagining, but our eyes are drawn past the gates to the little hill with the main road leading up to the rest of the city. A group, a large one.

Breeders, a big crowd of them.

A yell of delight and welcome goes up from the crowd.

But something is wrong. They're moving too fast, the way they're running . . .

They're being chased.

The city defence has finally mustered. They will be coming, though we can't see them yet, marching down the same road we did. We work our way to the front of the crowd, and after a moment another cry goes up as the rest realise the breeders are running from something.

The breeders are moving slow, and I feel a burst of irritation with their flowing cloth, their long hair. We can see the fear in their faces now. We watch as they look over their shoulders to gauge the distance between them and their enemies.

Run, I urge. *Don't look back.*

And now, topping the hill and rushing towards us, come management.

They are led by Guards; formed up, moving fast. Some banshees with them; it's hard to make out. Behind them, a straggle: mostly men, management, farmers, some breeders, even some wallers. All on the make,

I suppose, and I can't hate them for it. I grit my teeth. But we'll kill them if we have to.

I have time, while they come, to think how strange it is. Management would put their hands around our throats and choke us instead of opening up their fingers: they would be in control, till we threaten them back, and then they'd risk their own lives as well as ours for this control.

Many of the men carry sticks, shovels, whatever they have fantasised about murdering us with. Their banshees, management-loyal, will have their weapons. They'll have whatever they wanted. They'll be armed with knives, and I'm the only one in this small crowd with a knife good enough for throwing.

Agata, where are you? Smoke is still billowing from the south-east.

The breeders are closing on the gates but the guards and the banshees – call them all Guards from now, if that's what they want to be – they are coming up faster.

'Close the gates!' I shout.

It is the right thing to do. There is no point letting die those who can escape. No point protecting those who are already dead.

Aoife and Lin shout it too and the cry is taken up.

I tear my gaze from the breeders, tripping and falling,

some with babies in their arms, to the pack behind them, to the gates, which are slowly, creakily, closing.

'Get to the tunnel!' I shout, hoping that this cry will be taken up too. One of the men shouldering the huge, heavy gate meets my eye, and he nods.

The breeders, they're doing well, moving fast.

I look back at the gate, move closer to the men. 'Leave one open! Wait as long as you can!'

Before he can nod again I run forwards to get back to Aoife and Lin and anyone else hoping to mount a defence. Precious few.

I reach for my knife.

Aoife and Lin check each other over.

It's time to do what we were meant for.

I feel bodies on either side of me and look to my left, my right: the men from the gate, letting others take up their space behind the gate, risking their lives further to help us.

'Hello, fellas,' Aoife says, smiling flirtily, and I love her for it.

'May as well meet them at it,' I say.

'You're such an asshole,' Lin tells me. 'I never liked you.'

We rush forwards and at first it's just us. Then the stream of the quickest of the breeders, faces full of fear but determination too, get by us, and as I glance back I see some of them at least will make it through the last open gate. Men there waiting to grab them through.

'Here,' I say. We can get into position better from a standing start, better than running at them.

I hear a great thwack and zing and flinch to my right – a knife, I think, whizzing past my head. The Guards will fire on us first. Once we are dealt with, they can take their time doing whatever management ordains with the breeders. They'll pry open these gates and kill whoever they can.

More breeders move past us and we shout at them to keep moving, but we don't have to tell them anything. All we have to do is hold management off, I think, and it feels like we might, though my death is in there somewhere. This time, at last, I am not going to make it. There's too many. They'll mow through us and then they'll get through the gates and they'll chase after the others, through the tunnels, out to the beaches, all the way to Slanbeg. And for the first time it becomes clear to me that all we can do is try to slow them. Take as many of them with us as we can.

If I survive, I think, I'll make sure Agata is OK. And then I'll find the woman with the face and her child, and make sure they're OK. I'll find my knives, if they can be found in this city. I'll dig up the bones of Maeve and I'd carry her all the way back to the island.

I want to live, still. Despite it all.

I look to my left, my right, see the tense, beloved faces of Aoife and Lin. The men with us for no other reason than the good in their hearts. I close my eyes and picture the rest with us – Agata, Sene and Mare, little Jay too. A last time. I hear my mothers calling me home.

Here come the banshees, streaking ahead of the weapon-wielding men.

It's B-Troop.

I think about letting go of my knife. I could get Saoirse from here. At last. But once it's gone, it's gone. I hang tight: nothing for us to do but wait. I hold firm.

They get to us with a final burst of speed and then stop, Saoirse stopping, laying down her pack in front of her. Turning to face the rest.

'C'mon, A-Troop!' she shouts at us over her shoulder. 'Or whatever's left of it. Useless *fucking* shower.'

Then she looks again. Tips me a grin. I give her the finger.

'Form up!'

We form up with B-Troop, turning to face the fight together.

We've moments till the rest are on us, but there's nearly a dozen of us now to face the horde. I feel a stirring of hope.

They've slowed, I realise. The men with their tools,

whatever banshees are with them, they've been given pause.

The last of the group of breeders get by us.

'Go with them,' I say to the gate-man. 'Lock it after you.'

He nods.

'Hey!' I shout.

He looks back.

'Thank you.'

He's gone, the big, handsome shape of him.

The others are on us.

In a close-quarter combat event like this with multiple enemies it's best to go for the weakest first. Get the numbers down, thin them out.

The first two men go down well. I'm using my metal bar for range but it's good to know I've my knife still. I'm flung to the ground by a well-placed swing from one of the bigger ones, but Aoife and Lin are nearby and it's a moment's work to them to take him out. The weight of him lands on me and it takes a minute to work my way out from under, winded as I am. I'm just standing again, righting myself, when someone catches me. I barely register the pain, but feel a sharp thump, almost like a taste, in the depths of my nose.

I'm out.

I'm never quite gone; the darkness I inhabit is too spiky and uncomfortable to be death. It hurts. Coming to takes time. I hear noises and after a while I register they are voices, but it's longer still till I can grasp what they're saying. By this time my eyes are open. Once the voices come into focus the shapes around me begin to do so as well.

I'm still on the little battlefield where we pitched our fight to try and save the breeders. Around us lie corpses. Cin and Liara – I struggle upright, no, Aoife and Lin – a hand on my shoulder.

'We're here, you're OK,' Aoife tells me.

I breathe.

'The fight?'

'We did OK,' Saoirse says, 'no thanks to you.'

'Most of them fled, some men dead and a couple of Guards,' Lin tells me.

I look to the east. Smoke visible still. Black.

'We have to get out of here,' I mumble, and then say it louder, clearer.

'Stay a moment, you're OK,' Aoife says.

'No,' I say. 'How long was I out?' I dig into her upper arm with my fingers. 'How long?'

'Not long,' Aoife says. 'Look – enough for all the blood in that guy to run out of him. No longer.'

I stand up woozily.

'Agata,' I say. 'She wants to let in the skrake.'

'What?' Lin says, and I know by the look of her, and

Aoife, that they knew as much about this as I did.

'She started that fire over by the old city doors,' I say. 'She was trying to burn them down so the skrake could get in. Ash—'

'What about Ash?' Saoirse says, coming closer.

'She tried to stop Agata,' I say. 'Ash is dead.'

'Good,' Saoirse said.

'We have to move,' Lin says.

Aoife nods and holds out her hands to me.

The gates are closed tight and we pull to see can we get them to budge. The man did a good job. I get to work with my metal bar, but wedging it between the shut gates is tricky.

'Find something I can use!' I shout at the others standing around me.

There's a quality to the silence of them that makes me stop.

Turn.

I let my eyes scan the horizon, up the small slope in the near-distance we were so afraid would bring down management upon us.

On the ridge, a shape. Moving in a way we all know.

'Shit, that's Ash's pet,' Saoirse says.

'That's OK,' says Aoife. 'One little skrake, easy.'

'Form up,' I say, as a matter of course, just as Saoirse says the same thing to her troop.

And then, from the east.

More movement.

'Oh fuck.'

'The doors.'

I turn back to the gates, trying to wedge my bar somehow, to pull.

The skrake will move fast. They'll move so fast and there'll be so many of them.

'Orpen!' A shout, from far off. I look up.

It's Agata, sprinting towards us from the direction of the tunnels.

'We need the key!' I shout at her. 'Do you have the key?'

She stops running.

'The key!' I shout again.

She turns and runs.

'Fucking A-Troop scum,' Saoirse mutters beside me.

'Would you for once in your life—' Aoife starts.

'She's coming back,' I say. I look over my shoulder. 'Stay very still, stay quiet.'

It's just possible they hadn't seen us yet, that they are spreading throughout the city, cold and impersonal as frost.

But they move so quickly. Straight for us.

'Some can escape,' I say, thinking quickly. 'We can give each other boosts, make a chain, maybe get a couple of us over, save—'

'Orpen!'

Agata is running back for us, holding something in one hand.

She's with us in moments. We fumble getting the gate open, getting the key to turn. It takes time for us all to slip through, to lock it again tight.

The skrake reach for us through the bars. They'll get through, but not today.

Agata holds me close, whispering, 'I'm sorry. I'm sorry.'

Epilogue

FOUR DAYS ON THE ROAD.

Foot sore and heartsick, leaving the city smoking behind us.

Twice we are attacked, our flanks rushed by no more than two at a time, nothing A-Troop can't handle on its own. I was so keen to protect on the road, but walking with the city-dwellers, safe, I feel misplaced.

We lose only two, a man who had been injured getting out, and a child, no more than a year, who had never been well. It did not make it easier, burying his little body on the side of the road. We stand around them together, the big grave and the small, but even mourning with the others, I feel that feeling that I'm not one of them.

We hear, gathered in the evenings, in whispered conversations, horror stories of what happened in those last hours in the city, of those being kept prisoner, those who had to fight. Heroics. And loved ones left behind.

We encourage each other. Not long now till we can speak free.

Agata, for the first and last time, tries to explain herself to me as we walk. She tries in different ways.

'There was no way we could do it otherwise,' she says.

'The skrake would have got us,' she says.

'See all these children?' she says.

I don't think she's wrong exactly.

It was Agata, of course, herself and Cat, running around injuring men. They'd plotted for years to disable whatever men whispers led them to believe needed to be disabled. They knew there'd be a chance, one way or another, to let in the skrake eventually, or at least set Ash's pet free. And the men who were hobbled would be got first. And whoever else, whoever would not or could not leave with us, would be got too.

For better or worse, their plans worked: we got out. Some of us.

I don't think she's right either. I think mostly she was desperate and angry.

I glance at her now, talking quietly to the women next to her ahead of me, smiling, never looking back. When she's not with me or Cat, she's up there leading. She remembers the way to the beach.

We've difficulties to face, still. We've to find a way for all of us to get to the island. We've problems getting everyone enough water even though, as we move further west, it rains more. There are hungry bellies already.

But we've enough time for that now. I rejoice in everyone alive around me; the gate-man, Phelim, B-Troop. The woman who silently put the house's food in our bowls twice a day every goddam day I was in the city. Her name is Flo.

There is no young woman with a scarred face amongst us. There's no little girl belonging to her, though I'm not sure I'd recognise the child now if I saw her.

The day comes when we find ourselves on a beach I am familiar with, a stretch of sand and rock Agata has seen once before. We stand on the dunes of Battle Beach for a moment together. The mist is beyond us, laying thick on the sea and hiding the island well.

There is no skiff and I think about what that means.

If Cillian and the others, the runaways I met on the road so long ago, if they made it to the island, could they be there still? I add it to the other questions I cannot stop repeating, especially now. Was it better I stayed on the island altogether? Did I do what Mam would have wanted, and Maeve? Should I have left quietly like they did, and how many died because I did not, how many died because, how many how many—

We make camp on the beach, sheltering best we can amongst the dunes, finding places to make cook-fires while it's still light and they've less chance of attracting skrake. We all feel an attack now is more likely, days away from Dublin.

We watch the children play along the shore, quiet and careful still, but getting bolder by the day. Watching them, so intent on the present moment, helps all of us.

Some of the banshees stay with the camp while the rest of us go looking for boats on missions that take us away for a night and, once, two. It is the last time Agata and I work as a team and I try to enjoy that as best I can. I try to make sure I appreciate her and all she has done for me.

Further north we find three boats and we row them back to Battle Beach with driftwood and branches, hugging the coast. We are welcomed with relief and rainwater. I'm left alone to sit in the sand dunes watching Cat direct the camp as it's broken and put carefully on the boats. I try to imagine the delight at finding houses mostly intact, a whole village and a housing estate, the dusty rooms of a school.

I try not to imagine the people left in my own little house, coming out, surprised, when they hear voices on the beach.

Agata strides up to me, legs long and strong and dark against the pale of the dunes. Her teeth white. She smiles all the time now; I can't stand it. She pauses for a moment, shielding her eyes so she can look at the beach, then looking back at me. 'I think Phelim is in love with you,' she says.

'Who is Phelim?'

She laughs and sits so we're almost touching, and brushes the sand off her hands. I've to work at it not to inch away.

'The man you named after a gate,' she says, picking under her nails. 'I won't miss that.'

'The sand?'

'Gets everywhere.'

'There still might be people there,' I blurt. 'There could still be people hiding.'

'Anybody who had stairs to get up doesn't deserve to be rescued.'

'We'd stairs, Agata,' I say. I'm stunned by her. One of these days I'll have to stop being surprised by the turns she takes.

She snorts. 'We may as well have been underground already. Nobody gave a shit whether we lived or died.'

I shake my head, tears welling. We had it better than most people in the city, bad as things were for us.

'I know you're not coming,' she says.

'It's not that I don't want to.' I take a big breath, try to calm down, to be less angry with her. 'But it'd take all afternoon, to get to the island, and back again. People might be dying in the meantime. I'm sorry,' I say, and I am. 'I only came this far in case of attacks.'

'Could still be attacks,' she says. Sounding a little unsure of herself.

'I owe debts, still,' I say, thinking of Maeve's bones. 'There's a woman with a daughter whose house we tore down, in the shanties. I haven't been able to stop thinking about her.'

'You've been a little far away,' Agata says. 'I thought it was that twinge in your side you've been getting—'

'That's gone from me,' I say.

'Or, you know, Cat.'

I stop short and we look at each other. 'You should have told me,' I say, but there's no anger in my voice. It seems a little thing now, against everything else.

'It's just, if I told you that, there'd have been a lot of other things to tell you too. And I know Ash could be so persuasive . . .'

'It's OK,' I say, and I mean it. 'I like her.'

'No, you don't,' Agata laughs.

'No, I don't,' I say, shaking my head.

'You're coming back?'

I nod. If I can find survivors I'll need to take them somewhere.

'Like your woman with the baby,' she says. 'Whoever is left will have had to survive a week.'

'I can be back in two days if I work through the night.'

'And if nobody is left?'

'At least I'll know,' I say. 'Leave a skiff out for me if you can. You know the way?'

'You've told me it. Seems easy.'

'It is. Straight out, under the bridge. Keep going till your hands are raw. Come back to the beach if you get stuck and try again, but probably you just haven't gone far enough.'

She nods and asks suddenly, 'Should I go with you?' She turns to face me, her eyes steady on mine.

Agata would come if I asked her to, I realise. I smile and shake my head. Partners are only worth something if you can trust them.

'You're a good one,' she tells me seriously.

My eyes well up again. I had never considered that before.

Agata puts her arms around me and I hold her close, smelling her good, rich smell. I feel good. I feel that I have tried my best. I'm glad there's still more trying to do.

I allow myself to linger, to watch the boats leave,

slowly and haphazardly as the women and men get used to the oars and the children try to help, or shout at the surprise of being floated on the water.

I walk down to the beach and see there's a pile left for me: a sparker, a canteen, a tarp, a good backpack, one of the ones we took from the airport, days ago – a lifetime ago.

Undeserved riches.

The boats disappear, gulped down by the mist and I persuade myself that even if they can't find their way to the island right away, they'll be all right. I shoulder the backpack.

Towards my knives, if I can find them. Towards saving, if I can, anyone that's left.

Towards finding the bones of my mother, bringing them home to rest.

I am moving.

Acknowledgements

I'll never not feel my luck in being published by out-standing publisher and editor Mary-Anne Harrington at Tinder Press in the UK. Thank you so much, Mary-Anne, and thank you Ellie Freedman.

I can't thank everyone at Flatiron enough, especially to Christine Kopprasch. Thanks also to Maxine Charles, Samantha Zukergood, and jacket designer Phil Pascuzzo.

Particular thanks to my exceptional agent Sallyanne Sweeney. I know how lucky I am to benefit from the work of the excellent team at Mulcahy Sweeney Literary Agency and I'm grateful to Marc Simonsson, Adrienn Arvai, Donna Wilson, Edwina de Charnace, Stephanie Coen and especially to Ivan Mulcahy.

Thanks to the brilliant team at Treasure Entertainment.

Living and working in Ireland I'm indebted to the Hachette Ireland publicity team, particularly Elaine Egan.

I'm very grateful to have benefitted from two stays at the Tyrone Guthrie Centre which made meeting deadlines (or only just missing them) possible.

Thanks to my parents Robert and Sheelagh Davis-Goff for providing support in pretty much all the ways it's possible to do so.

Thanks and love to my brothers William, Henry and James and sister-in-law Sarah, to whom this book is dedicated.

Thanks to friends, and to encouraging readers – Rebecca Wardell, Susie Hill, Louise Hodgson, Marco Herbst, Deirdre Sullivan and Diarmuid O'Brien, Rick O'Shea and Liz Lyons, Louise O'Neill, Sophie White. A particularly big thanks to Roe McDermott who edited an early draft, helping me immeasurably.

I really appreciate the support and understanding of Lisa Coen.

The biggest of all thanks to Dave, and to Sammy.